baby DADDY

KENDALL RYAN

Baby Daddy
Copyright © 2018 Kendall Ryan

Content Editing by
Becca Hensley Mysoor
Elaine York

Copy Editing and Formatting by
Pam Berehulke

Proofreading by
Virginia Tesi Carey

Cover Design by
Uplifting Designs

All rights reserved. No part of this book may be reproduced or transmitted in any form without written permission of the author, except by a reviewer who may quote brief passages for review purposes only.

This book is a work of fiction. Names, characters, places, and incidents are either the product of the author's imagination or are used fictitiously.

About the Book

We met in a trapped elevator.

Emmett was on his way to work, sophisticated and handsome in his tailored suit and tie.

I was on my way to the sperm bank. Awkward, right?

At thirty-five, my life hadn't taken the path I thought it would and I was tired of waiting—I wanted a baby. And I was ready to take matters into my own hands to make it happen.

After our ill-fated elevator encounter, Emmett insisted on taking me to dinner—he also insisted on something else—that I ditch my plan involving a turkey baster and let him do the job. He would be my baby daddy. He was a wealthy and powerful CEO with little interest in diapers or playdates. And since he didn't want kids, I'd be on my own once his bun was in my oven, free to go my own way.

But once his baby was inside me, it was like a switch had been flipped, and I got a whole lot more than I ever bargained for.

Prologue

Emmett

I love my dick.

That's a fact.

And I'm not afraid to admit he's both my best friend and my most trusted advisor. Sure, he's gotten me into some tight spots over the years—pun very much intended—but that's what makes life fun, right? I wouldn't trade our relationship for the world. He stands tall and proud . . . and when he spots something he likes? He bobs with pleasure, begging to get closer.

And as for me? Well, I trust his judgment. Completely. He didn't bob for the stunning and funny Laura in accounting. I knew there was a reason, and as it turns out, she's a bit of a klepto. Three hundred seventy-two staplers kind of klepto.

But I'm not a total douchebag, I promise. I'm just a young CEO under immense pressure, so in my downtime, blowing off steam is practically a necessity. It's my duty to keep my dick happy, and a steady diet of beautiful women keeps us both satisfied. I do what I can to make his life as simple and as easy as possible. Plenty of no-strings sex does the trick.

I find that when he's well taken care of, I feel better and my brain works efficiently. Shit, my whole life just seems easier.

It's that simple. I love my dick, and loving my dick makes my entire life better.

When my dick perks up in interest, begging for a taste of the woman we're stranded with in a stuck elevator for two hours, I listen to his dirtiest wishes and ask her out to dinner. But the last thing I expect her to say is that she's not interested in my dick. She's just interested in the stuff inside, the stuff that can give her the baby she so desperately wants. No strings attached.

Who am I to say no?

Welcome to the craziest ride my dick's ever gotten me into.

Chapter One

Jenna

This is it.

This skyscraper doesn't look like anything special. No different from any of this city's dozens of office buildings covered in mirrored windows or gray concrete. But as soon as I cross the threshold, I'll be taking the first step toward my dream.

Every step feels heavy with anticipation. I pause outside the building's tall revolving door, steeling my nerves for what I'm about to do. This is just a consultation, I tell myself. It's not like I'm getting knocked up right here on the spot. They probably won't even prescribe me any fertility drugs yet. All I'm doing is getting more information and learning how the process works. Still, it feels more like I'm jumping off a cliff rather than walking into a doctor's office.

Smoothing my sweaty hands over my skirt, I take a deep breath to chase away the butterflies in my stomach. Then I stride inside and cross the lobby. I've never been so excited or so frightened. There's no doubt in my mind that this is what I want, but having a baby is still a monumental decision. It's not like it's a pair of shoes I can return if I have buyer's remorse. I can't take it back, and it will change my life forever.

In the elevator, I press the button for the thirteenth floor. There's something that strikes me as ominous with that floor number. But I know that it's just my nerves and anxiety working overtime, so I step in.

Just before the doors close, a large, strong-looking hand shoves between them and they retreat. A man in a crisp navy suit and a white shirt steps inside—and damn, *what* a man. My jaw threatens to drop open at the mouthwatering sight. He's tall, with broad shoulders that his tailored jacket does nothing to hide. Sculpted jaw. Dark hair in a clean-cut, classic style. Brown eyes, the color of a rich brandy, with just a few lines around them crinkle at the corners in mischief.

I hastily pretend to be fascinated with the carpet so he doesn't catch me ogling him. He hits the button for the top floor and stands a little closer than necessary.

Is he doing that on purpose? Does he not understand the concept of personal space, especially when his personal space is practically rubbing up against mine? No, he's acting perfectly normal; I'm the one who's reading way too much into this situation. Damn these nerves.

I can't turn off my awareness of him. I can smell his crisp cologne. Hell, if I didn't know better, I'd swear I can feel his body heat. My heart beats faster as we rumble upward, floor by floor, the tiny enclosed space of the elevator just full of him. Even though he hasn't said a word, his presence is still so intense, almost overpowering.

Dammit, he's perfect.

It's ridiculous how scorching hot he is and how I've run into him here, now, of all times and places. It's almost like the universe is laughing at me. Mocking my decision to give up on finding a partner to plant his seed in my garden of love. Dangling the exact kind of man I've always wanted—and never managed to catch—right in front of me. He even looks about my age, maybe a few years older. I sneak another glance and peg him at mid to late thirties. *This is so unfair.*

Suddenly, there's a metallic screech. A jolt that makes us both stumble. Our breaths catch simultaneously, and his hands reach out and grab my upper arms. I'm seared by his touch. Every part of me is alive.

My eyes fly open wide. *No. No, seriously, come on. You gotta be kidding me.*

Ignoring my frantic prayers, the elevator grinds to a jarring halt.

"Shit," the man grumbles. "You all right?" His gaze penetrates mine, and I'm unsure if the tightness in my stomach is because of his touch or because of the elevator.

I nod. "Just startled." *And a bit pissed off.* Although, despite everything, I still can't help noticing that his voice is just as yummy as the rest of him. A smooth, rich baritone.

Rather than pressing the HELP button on the wall panel, he releases his hold on me and pulls out his phone. "Hey, Ted. The elevator's stopped." A pause. "Does it matter? Somewhere around the tenth floor." A much longer pause, during which a deep furrow appears in his brow that causes my stomach to sink. "I see. Thanks." He hangs up.

"Well?" I ask, unable to keep the anxiety from my voice.

"That was the building maintenance manager. He's going to call a repair crew, but he said it'll probably be about half an hour until the company can get them dispatched, and then at least another half hour until they can fix whatever the problem is." The man pockets his phone, looking annoyed but unconcerned. "Looks like we're stuck here for a while."

Meanwhile, I groan, wanting to tear my hair out. "Ugh, I can't believe this."

Good-bye, doctor's appointment. Hello, no-show fee and redoing all the scheduling hassle. Maybe they'll waive the fee, at least. I have a good excuse—they're sure to hear about their own building's elevator breaking down. Thank God I ate breakfast this morning.

Oh my God. Why am I thinking about breakfast right now when my nerves have scrambled—pun intended—every breakfast morsel sitting in my stomach. I almost feel like vomiting.

"Yeah, it's a pain in the ass." He sighs. "But there's

nothing we can do about it now besides make ourselves comfortable." He lowers himself to sit cross-legged on the floor, expensive suit and all.

How can he be so blasé about being trapped in a metal box for an hour, possibly longer? Me, I'm trying to get my anxiety together and not lose my shit.

I cock my head at him. "You don't have somewhere to be?"

"Yes, work, but my office will probably be happy that I'm showing up late for once." He chuckles. "My name's Emmett, by the way."

When I don't make a move to sit, he gives me another smile. "I promise I don't bite. Not unless you ask nicely. Join me?"

God, why does he have to be so fucking hot? And whatever *this* is—this flirty banter from him? I'm so out of practice, it's not even funny. What do I do with my hands right now?

I awkwardly kneel on my side of the elevator, holding down my skirt so I don't flash him by accident. "I'm

Jenna. So, you work in this building? What do you do?"

I guess we have nothing better to do right now than strike up a conversation. And talking is the only thing that will keep me from obsessively texting my assistant, Britt, to ask how she's handling things at the bookshop.

He shrugs. "I took over the family business a couple of years ago."

Way to avoid actually answering what it is that he does for a living. *This is going to be a long hour.*

In that moment, his friendly smile turns crooked. He glances at the button I punched on the control panel. "And what about you? You were headed to the spank bank?"

My head pulls back as I open and close my mouth a few times, struck dumb. "What? It's . . . I . . . No!"

"Sorry, that's a pretty juvenile term, I suppose." He smirks at me. "Masturbation station? I'm sure that's not much better." His smirk is overwhelmingly sexy.

I roll my eyes for good measure. "I'm not going there. And even if I were, it's none of your business," I

Baby Daddy 13

say with a huff, hoping my cheeks aren't turning pink.

His grin is full-on devilish now. "The clinic is the only thing on that floor, so you were either going there for business ... or for pleasure. You aren't carrying a big enough briefcase to be a pharmaceutical rep, you don't look old enough to be a jizz doctor, and you aren't dressed in scrubs, so you aren't a nurse. There's only one option left."

I'm rescued from further interrogation by my phone ringing. *Thanks for the save, Mom.*

"Hold on, I should take this," I mutter, then turn aside slightly to answer. "Hello?"

"Did they stick it in yet?" Mom hollers without preamble. "Or do they just give you the stuff in a little jar?"

Did I say thanks to the woman who birthed me? I take it all back.

I keep my phone volume on maximum, and Mom's voice is permanently set to "as loud as humanly possible." Glancing at Emmett, I see he's smirking like he's holding in a laugh.

Fuck, my face is on fire. "N-now's not a good time, Mom. I'm stuck in an elevator."

"Oh no! You spent weeks trying to get that appointment. What a shame. Are you okay? Did you bring a snack? Do you need to pee?"

I love you very much, but please shut up. "It's fine, seriously," I hiss through gritted teeth. "A repair crew's coming to get us out any minute now. I'll call you later."

"But what about your—"

"SorryIloveyoubye." I hammer the END CALL button before she can announce more embarrassing details to the world, then grudgingly glance back at ungodly sexy Emmett. "Any chance you didn't hear that?"

He shakes his head, still smirking. "Sorry, I'm not going to lie. I heard every word, and my question has been answered. Pleasure, it is."

"Awesome." I drop my phone back into my purse and consider dying on the spot.

There's a moment of silence before Emmett says,

"So, that seems like a—"

"Yes, okay? You were right." I sigh. "I'm going to the fertility clinic. I want a baby. It's not a big deal." But, of course, it is a big deal. The biggest.

"There's nothing wrong with that. But why didn't your husband come with you? Seems inconsiderate to let you do this all alone."

Ouch. "Because I don't have one."

"Your boyfriend, then."

I shake my head. "Fresh out of those too."

He blinks, surprised. "Girlfriend?"

Dear God, this man . . . "No. I'm single." Maybe not always happily, but I think I'm doing all right. Except for times like this, sitting near a prime male specimen like Emmett and having to look and not touch. I really want to touch. Even just to strangle him.

"I see." He rubs his chin, looking thoughtful. "So you're just . . . doing it."

I give him a curt nod. "Yup."

A heavy silence hangs between us, and his gaze latches onto mine like he's trying to sort this out, trying to understand it—understand *me*—on some deeper level. I fiddle with my hands in my lap, not exactly pleased that his knitted brow suggests I'm a complicated math equation—or a bomb he needs to defuse.

Clearing my throat, I square my shoulders, fighting to regain some of the confidence I've lost since the elevator stopped. "I'm sorry, this is . . . can we just start over?"

Emmett raises both hands in front of him. "Yes, absolutely. I didn't mean to pry. I'm sure it's a very personal decision."

I nod again. "It is. It's just . . ."

I take a deep gulp of air and let my gaze wander to the beige paneled walls. It seems the perfect metaphor—I'm tired of living a beige life. I want more.

"I'm used to taking the bull by the horns," I say, my voice rising. "I started my own business a few years ago, and it's left little time for relationships. Now I'm thirty-five, and . . ." *The clock is ticking.* I shake my head. "I guess it's not that out of character for me, going after something

I want. I've made all the big life decisions up till now, so this is really no different."

Except that it is. It's very different, and doesn't just involve me if I fail.

Why am I telling him all this? When I left the house this morning, I never expected to have to bare my soul to a stranger. Then again, no one's forcing me. Perhaps it's just a byproduct of being trapped together in such close proximity with the scent of his cologne lingering in the air. Smelling him, inhaling him, it's like drinking truth serum.

"You're an independent woman. I think it's admirable." Emmett smiles warmly, and I feel the flutter of butterfly wings again.

It's nice to have someone acknowledge my decision. Especially someone who seems so normal and levelheaded. My biggest fear in all of this is being judged—by family, by friends, by strangers like him—being made to feel like a nut case for living life on my own terms. I'm glad to see that's not the case. At least, not by Emmett's standards.

"You don't happen to have a deck of cards or

something in that bag of yours, do you?" he asks.

I'm so thankful we've moved on from the topic of my uterus that my shoulders feel an actual weight lift off of them.

"Sadly, no." I slip my purse off my shoulder and open it in my lap, scrounging around for anything that will keep the subject off of my life choices. "Would you like a cough drop?" I pull out a handful of the cherry-flavored drops that have been tumbling around at the bottom of my purse since last winter.

He chuckles. "I'm good."

Together, Emmett and I begin taking stock of our personal inventory to pass the time, and I'm amazed at how casual it feels being stuck here with him. I'm not thinking about my assistant, the shop, or the doctor who's probably wondering where I am right now. There's no panic, no rush to get out.

We set everything on the floor between us. I pull out a package of tissues, a pen, mint chewing gum, hand sanitizer, and six tubes of lipstick. He contributes his smartphone and the key fob to a Mercedes, joking that we'd be screwed in a zombie apocalypse if we needed to survive on these meager items, all the while vowing to stockpile better supplies for any future catastrophes such as this.

"Wait." My fingers feel around in the zippered compartment, and I locate a mini-sized candy bar. "Ta-da!"

"Wow. Not bad. Except for the fact that nobody likes Three Musketeers. It's all nougat. And it's squished. Seriously, how long have you carried that around in there?"

I frown at him. "I happen to like nougat, and beggars shouldn't be choosy. If this were a real crisis, you'd be begging me for some."

With that, he glances up at me and raises his right brow, a silent innuendo unspoken between us . . . one that doesn't involve chocolate or nougat but rather something deliciously more sinful. *Jesus, why is my mind immediately going to the gutter here?*

He sighs with a knowing smile. "And here I was starting to think you were totally normal and might like a little begging."

Needing to change the subject again, I snatch my candy bar from the pile, bumping our knees together. "I was going to share it with you, but never mind."

Emmett gives me another of those playful megawatt grins, then absently picks up the tubes of lipstick, opening each one in turn and raising the stick to inspect the color. "Which is your favorite?"

I shrug. "Depends on my mood."

Emmett looks at a soft pink, almost nude-colored lipstick, raising a brow.

"That's an everyday color. I usually wear it to work."

"Or to doctor's appointments at the fertility clinic."

He's observant. I'm wearing that shade now. "Yes."

"I like it." His voice is deeper, huskier somehow, and he's still looking at my mouth.

The tension and chemistry that have been building between us rise to a new all-time high. An image of me climbing on top of him flashes through my mind, and I have to look away. This feels an awful lot like flirting, and a little bit like foreplay. Plucking my favorite tube from the pile, I show him the bright hue that's between a pink and a red.

"This one is made more for evening, and it's typically the one I'd wear on a date."

Why did I just tell him that? God, what is it about this man that makes me prone to spill my secrets? It's official. I'm truly pathetic.

At this, he stops fidgeting and his eyes meet mine, an intensity to them that I haven't yet seen in our elevator rendezvous. "I like that idea."

"What idea?" My mind comes to a screeching halt and my shoulders tense.

"Just hear me out for a second." He recaps the lipstick and hands it to me. "About the whole baby-making thing . . . what would you say to going on a date with me first?"

I blink at him. "Well, I think the first thing I'd say would be, *huh*? And the second would be, *why*?"

"What do you mean, why? You're a gorgeous woman." He turns his palm up, as if proposing a business deal. "Just think about it. Before you do this, let me take you to dinner and see if you're interested in trying . . . the old-fashioned way instead." His eyes smolder.

I immediately do this awkward gasp-choke thing, my breath coming out faster than my lungs will tolerate. I stare wide-eyed at Emmett and immediately think that the oxygen in the elevator must be depleted, causing us both to say and do things we normally wouldn't.

Once I've gotten my breathing under control, I look up at him, my mind reeling with a response. "You want to help me?"

"With my sperm, yes. I mean, we'll work out the details later. But, what do you have to lose? I have a college education. My family doesn't have any serious medical issues that we know of. I'm athletic . . . got third place all-state with my high school track team." His voice is so nonchalant. "Not to mention, I'm pretty damn good in bed."

My brain crashes and explodes. I stare at him, openmouthed. Is he saying what I think he's saying? I can't think of any other way to interpret his words. This smoking-hot man wants to fuck me. He's offering to *put a baby in me.*

Holy shit, what? We've known each other a whole half hour. Not that I would know any of the men from the binder at the sperm clinic, but still.

Either ignoring or not noticing my internal meltdown, Emmett continues. "And if you decide you're not feeling it and you'd truly rather use the clinic, then no harm done. Go right ahead. Hell, if you want company, I'll even hold your hand while they put in the turkey baster and spread the nut butter."

"Oh my God . . . you know they don't use a turkey baster," I say, managing to correct him through my haze of shock and increasingly naughty thoughts, climbing on top of him right now being the tamest. "It's much more clinical, you know. They catheterize your cervix."

He winces. "Ouch. A couple of orgasms sounds much more fun to me." He raises his eyebrows at me insistently. "So, your verdict on dinner?"

My throat has gone bone dry. This man is throwing a

major curveball my way, and I'm not sure how to feel about that. I have everything set, but now he's right here in front of me, offering me more than I could ever hope for, and I'm silently considering it. Like seriously considering it. I'm blaming it on the low oxygen levels for what comes out of my mouth next.

"How about we grab coffee sometime?"

He shakes his head. "Coffee isn't a real date. Neither is anything else that happens before five p.m. or takes less than an hour. That's my personal policy." He looks resolute.

Even if we don't ever have mind-blowing sex, a date would be nice. I consider, then shrug, his smile coaxing out one of my own. "Sure. Dinner would be nice."

As if the universe was waiting for me to cave, the elevator groans and shudders to life, heading down as soon as we're done exchanging phone numbers.

The doors open up to the lobby and an apologetic repair crew. We thank them, then stand there awkwardly, watching each other.

"I'll look at my calendar and text you later," he says,

his voice low.

I nod. "Okay. Have fun at work."

Emmett nods and we part ways, him into another elevator and me out to the parking lot. I figure there's no point in visiting the clinic now. It might not be my fault, but I'm so embarrassed this whole debacle has made me so late, I've missed my entire appointment. And even if I hadn't missed it, I'd be too busy thinking about the crazy deal I just struck with a total stranger in a broken-down elevator to focus on anything the doctor said anyway.

God, I must be nuts. What the hell was I thinking? But somehow, I can't bring myself to regret agreeing to a date. Emmett calmed me when I would normally be panicking ... and that damn smirk? I'm certain that smirk has dropped countless panties across the entire state.

Heading back to the bookshop, I try to shake off the strange interlude in the elevator and get back to the real world. The whole thing was so surreal that I almost feel like I dreamed it, yet I know I didn't.

I don't have time to ponder this all day; there's a mountain of work waiting for me at the bookshop. Right now, what I need most is to sit down at my desk and clear my head with purchase orders and invoices. I'll call the clinic to reschedule my consultation later, after Emmett's proposal inevitably turns out to be a flop.

At the very least, I'll still get a nice dinner out with a devastatingly handsome man.

Chapter Two

Emmett

I head out of the elevator and straight to my corner office, no time to lose. At my desk, I catch a glimpse out the window of a familiar tiny figure crossing the parking lot. It's Jenna, walking back to her car.

A smile tugs at my lips and my dick reminds me how interested it is in her. I'm oddly pleased to see her go. Maybe because it means she's postponing her visit to the sperm bank until after she's given me a fair shot. Or maybe it's just nice to watch those hips sway, even from my distant bird's-eye view. Despite what little I know about her, the woman is damn ballsy, and I instantly like that about her. Even if she does like disgusting nougat.

And my mind instantly goes to my spreading the nougat from a chocolate bar on my dick and then watching her suck it clean. Yes, under those circumstances, I could very well grow to love nougat.

Remembering I'm at the office and certainly can't walk around with a hard-on, seeing as I have a ton of meetings, I jump into work mode. I don't get any more time to think about the cute mystery brunette from the elevator, though, because a gaggle of staff flood in, clamoring for my attention. Most of them are senior managers. My lingering good mood from meeting Jenna begins to sour.

I decide to start with the most immediately useful person—my assistant.

"Lisa," I call out over the babble, and everyone falls silent. "Please call all of this morning's appointments, apologize for my unexpected absence, and reschedule. And can you grab me some coffee? Thanks."

Lisa nods and zips out my door. One down, a dozen to go.

I go through the crowd to see what everyone else needs and get them hustling back to their offices to send me reports, fill shipments, consult lawyers, and focus their teams on the most pressing tasks. I can already feel a tension headache stirring behind my eyes.

As I work my way through a couple of emails, I settle on one in particular that makes my pulse pound faster. Lately, the majority of my stress can be pinned on one stubborn target. A tiny uptown bookseller, just across the city, that refuses to let us acquire them.

We desperately need this deal. We're acquiring as many small bookstores as we can get our hands on, trying to save not only Baxter Books, but the whole business model of big-box bookstore chains from extinction. And yet, despite our best efforts—and what should be a huge leverage difference working in our favor—our opponent won't budge an inch. They won't even give us a chance to negotiate.

So, naturally, everything around here is devolving into a clusterfuck.

It takes almost an hour until I've put out all the fires. Finally, after my team has gotten everything under control on their end, I have a moment of peace. I take a grateful gulp of coffee, open a report Lisa has printed out and set on my desk, and start reading the financial analyses. But I can't focus on the dry, dense words. My thoughts keep drifting back to the attractive woman I met in the elevator.

Well, half the morning is already down the tubes . . . I can let this report wait a few minutes longer. I'm the boss, after all. I take a moment to lean my chair back and reflect on the encounter.

Jenna. I don't even know her last name yet, but I've already learned enough to pique my curiosity. I know that I want her—in my bed, under me, on top of me, wherever she'll let me have her. We hardly exchanged much in the way of useful information or personal history, but mostly because I was so baffled by her situation.

My first impression of her was that she's a strong, smart, and of course, drop-dead beautiful woman. She can't possibly lack for dates, and yet there she was, on her way to start a family all by her lonesome. I'm shocked she's still unattached at all, let alone resorting to a sperm bank and single motherhood. She didn't seem opposed to dating or men.

What man would let a girl like her slip through their

fingers? There has to be a story behind her. And I can't wait to uncover it … among other things. My mind lingers on the memory of her body, her curves and long, shapely legs. The way our knees brushing sent electricity and warmth flying through me. The hint of creamy cleavage peeking from her blouse.

To tell the truth, I barely understand why she wants a baby so badly at all. I've always been a once-and-done kind of guy, and I make no apologies for that. I only have room for one "baby" in my life—my company.

I may not love my job, but I have a duty to the family business Dad started, and more importantly, to his employees who are now mine. That will never change. God knows my brother and sister were even less interested in taking over the company than I was. And I would never repeat Dad's mistake of ignoring his own wife and kids in favor of living at the office. It probably wasn't a lesson he intended to teach, but I learned from his example that marriage and family don't mix well with a demanding career. You can't do both without fucking one of them up. A man has to pick one or the other, and since I'm responsible for Baxter Books, that means staying single. I don't resent that; it's just a fact of life. Not to mention that bachelorhood hardly lacks for fun.

The thought of exactly how much fun it can be brings me back to Jenna. I wouldn't have to be part of all the stressful stuff of parenting, just the fun part. The naked body parts and orgasms part. I don't have to change my life and she doesn't have to change hers. There's a lot of fun to be had with a no-strings-attached relationship. She gets a baby, we both get laid, and everybody wins.

Well, there's no time like the present. If she's on my mind and my dick's perked up in interest, why not get the ball rolling right now? I pull out my phone and text Jenna.

You still up for that date?

I'm halfway through writing a memo before a *yes* flashes on my screen.

Hmm. Not much hint of her feelings there, but I can work with it. *When are you free?*

Roughly another ten minutes pass, then: *Wednesday night.*

That's the day after tomorrow. I'm pleased that she's

just as uninterested in wasting time as I am. *Works for me. You like Mexican food?*

This time the reply is immediate. *Crazy about it. You have a place in mind?*

I chuckle and text back: *I was thinking I could pick you up and surprise you.*

No sense skimping on playfulness, even for a fuck-buddy arrangement. That stuff's half the fun of a fling.

A very long pause before she responds: *I'd rather meet there, if you don't mind. Seven okay?*

Fair enough. She has no way of knowing I'm not an ax murderer, after all, so only a dick would push for her home address. *Sure, that's cool.*

I send her the restaurant's location, consider this situation for a moment, then add a final line: *Looking forward to getting to know you better.*

Less than five minutes pass before her reply. *You too.*

Smiling, I click off my phone. I haven't been this intrigued in a long time.

Chapter Three

Jenna

I'm nervous.

Despite it being a Wednesday night, all the spots along Twenty-Ninth Street are taken. But I don't mind parking around the corner and walking a block. The early October evening is crisp, with just a hint of a breeze, and the chatter of the dinnertime crowd sounds light and friendly. I could use a moment to compose myself. My stomach is tied in knots at the thought of having dinner with Emmett.

Well, not just dinner, if I'm being honest. It's his comment about putting a baby inside me the "old-fashioned way" that has left me on edge for the past two days.

I take a deep breath and click the button on my key fob to lock my car, and focus on the sound of my high-heeled boots clicking along the pavement. I was unsure what to wear to the restaurant—it's the first date I've been on in a long time. A simple oatmeal-colored tunic with leggings and tousled hair was the look I settled on after trying on half my closet in an anxious fit.

I stopped looking for Mr. Right altogether at some point last year. Some well-meaning friends told me that love would find me once I stopped looking. They lied. Fuckers.

But none of that matters right now. I've promised myself that no matter what happens, I'm the one in control. If I don't like Emmett (or the things he has to say), I can just march my behind (and my uterus) right back to the clinic.

I expected Emmett to wait inside the restaurant. Instead, I spot him standing on the sidewalk as I approach, his hands in the pockets of his slate-gray sport coat, the very picture of a cultured, confident big shot.

Damn, he's even more attractive than I remember. I half hoped to see him in his business suit again, but this five-o'clock-shadowed casual look is just as appealing. More appealing, maybe. His dark gray chinos and blue polo fit close enough that I can't resist a quick up-and-down look. He must have gone home to spruce up after work before coming here, and I appreciate the effort almost as much as the view. The man is hot.

Emmett smiles and my eyes snap up to meet his.

Oops. Hopefully he didn't catch me checking out the goods. I'm here to decide whether I want his sperm sample, not to grab his ass. Not to take him home with me. Not to let him fuck the living daylights out of me . . .

Well, at least, not yet.

My stomach flips and I yank the plug out of my imagination. "Uh, hi," I say, giving him a lame wave.

"Hello, Jenna," he says, sounding genuinely glad to see me. I feel the weight of his gaze as it travels over me, making me warm. "You didn't wear the lipstick."

For a moment, I'm baffled, and then I recall our elevator conversation. The color I told him was my favorite and that I generally saved for dates.

"It's not a real date." *Is it?*

"Right, of course." Emmett nods. "Did you have any trouble finding the place?"

"No, I just hit a little traffic. Sorry I'm late." It's been a long time since I had a date, and I suddenly feel rusty.

He shrugs. "Only by five minutes, no big deal. Do

you want to sit outside?"

"Sure, the weather's nice." I let him escort me to the door, through the bustling restaurant and back out to the patio. His hand sits on the small of my back the entire way.

When the waiter comes to our table, we order two bottles of Victoria beer and half a dozen *carne asada* tacos, and he quickly returns with our drinks. I sip my frosty brew, admiring the sunset in one direction and the traditional-style decor in the other, all adobe and turquoise. "I can't believe I've never heard of this place before."

"Just wait until our food arrives—I'm convinced they make the best tacos in the city. I come here all the time after a long day." He winks. "Or a late night."

A silver-haired man, not our waiter, brings a basket of tortilla chips and stone bowls of fresh salsa and guacamole to the table. As he sets down our appetizers, he says to Emmett, "Aren't you going to introduce me to your lady friend?"

"Jenna, this is Tomás. His family has owned this

restaurant for almost fifty years . . ."

Tomás gives Emmett a look of good-natured exasperation. "Twenty-three years, to be exact," he says to me. "The gringo comes here whenever he wants *real* food."

With a grin, Emmett jumps right into what is clearly a well-worn game. "Aren't you too old to still be running around waiting tables? You need to settle down, old man."

"Ah, you wish. Would you listen to this young snot's nonsense?" Tomás shoots an incredulous look at me, as if inviting me into their sparring match, before firing back at Emmett. "Speak for yourself. When are *you* going to settle down? I never see you here with the same woman twice."

My ears perk up despite myself. *Really? So he's a playboy, huh?* I guess I'm not shocked to hear that a man with Emmett's looks gets around some, and really, his private life is none of my business. But it's oddly disappointing to have his escapades confirmed. Maybe I just thought he was more mature than that.

I'm curious to hear how much more Tomás might let

slip, but Emmett just laughs and waves off the insult. "Mind your own business."

Tomás sighs, shaking his head with a wry smile. "Excuse me, ma'am, I'll leave you to your meal. Have a lovely night, you two."

Our waiter soon returns with a huge platter of tacos, steaming hot and wafting delicious scents of grilled steak, corn tortillas, and chili peppers. My mouth waters. Lunch was a long time ago, and Mexican food is one of my biggest weaknesses.

I bite into one of the tacos and don't bother holding back a moan of delight. "Oh my God, you were right. This is incredible."

"I'll be sure to tell Tomás you said that." Emmett chuckles as he picks up another taco.

We dig in with gusto, and I find that Emmett has a way about him—an easy charm—that makes me feel comfortable. There's no fumbling for topics or awkward silences, and for that, I'm incredibly grateful. Just like I was in the elevator.

As we eat, I learn that he's thirty-eight (but I

wouldn't have guessed it), his last name is Smith, that he grew up not far from here, he has two siblings, and his best friend is an attorney. It's all such normal stuff that part of me keeps waiting to uncover something horrible about him. Like how he secretly keeps all his toenail clippings or has twenty-four cats. It's hard to understand how he's not married with a couple of kids by now. The normal ones always go first.

For a while, we just focus on enjoying our delicious dinner, keeping the conversation light as we indulge. Our arms brush from time to time. Our knees bump under the small table. The entire time, I'm completely aware of him, my entire body tingling and alive.

Our conversation runs naturally from discussing the amazing food to comparing our other favorite restaurants in the city to speculating on how our state college will do in the upcoming football season.

I suddenly realize that I'm having a good time—actually, a fabulous time. I've almost forgotten how nice dating can be. Emmett's mellow vibe is contagious. There's no pressure here. Just chilling out, sharing a meal, shooting the breeze. And I even get some top-notch eye candy with my meal.

When we've demolished most of the tacos, Emmett wipes his mouth and asks, "So I never asked, what do you do?"

"Oh, I'm in collectibles. Antiques, that sort of thing," I answer vaguely before taking another purposely huge bite.

I used to love talking business. I was, and still am, proud of all the hard work I've done building my little specialty bookshop from the ground up. But the shop's recent downturn in business has soured the topic with anxiety, and the recent buyout offer has made it even worse. Besides, I've found that men sometimes turn squirrelly when I mention my success as a female entrepreneur. If this were a real first date, I would want to gauge whether Emmett is the kind of guy who's intimidated by ambitious women before I invest too much time in getting to know him.

I don't have to invest the time, I remind myself. Because this can't come anywhere near a real commitment. We might have had a fun couple of hours, but we're not trying to start any kind of personal relationship here. I'm evaluating him for something much more short-term. I'm not looking for a partner; I'm looking for a donor. So there's no point forcing the conversation into awkward corners. Win-win.

Emmett props his chin on his hand, leaning forward. His dark eyes examine me. "I've been dying to know . . . no offense, but how the hell are you still single?"

I almost laugh. I've been wondering the exact same thing about him. "That's a very good question. My friends think my standards are too high." But I'm not about to settle. High standards are a good thing, as far as I'm concerned.

He nods once, his eyes going more serious. "Hence, the clinic."

"Yep. Or the 'spank bank,' as you not so affectionately put it." I arch my eyebrows at him pointedly, although the effect is somewhat ruined by my smirk.

He holds up his hand as he grins back. "Trust me, I was putting it nicely. They once had a contest for new slogans. You should have heard the things people in my office came up with that week. Even my sweet sixty-year-old secretary got in on it. I can't unhear some of those things." He pauses, his mouth lifting in a mischievous grin, and for a moment, I wonder if he's going to continue. "You spank it, we bank it. You throttle it, we bottle it. Things like that."

"Oh my God." A hand clapped over my mouth barely contains my very unladylike snort-laugh. And then my brain starts working. "You jack it, we pack it," I say with a giggle.

"That's actually pretty good." Emmett chuckles along with me. Then his smile fades as he continues watching me from across the table. "I think it's commendable, taking matters into your own hands, but what I still don't understand is, why have a baby at all?"

The muscles between my shoulders tense just a little. That question is much harder. I play with my beer bottle while I think, picking at the paper label. Finally, I reply, "I don't really know. Can anyone explain why they want to be a mother? I just do. I always have, ever since I was a kid myself. I could always feel something missing from my life. It's almost like . . . a calling."

I expect a blank stare, at best, and laughter, at worst. Instead, Emmett regards me with a serious, inquiring expression.

"I can't say I understand, but I'll take your word for it. I've got to say, that takes some grit to stare single motherhood in the face and say, 'Bring it on.'"

I flush and shrug off the unexpected compliment. "I'm no braver than millions of other women in the world. I couldn't put it off any longer, that's all. I knew I wanted a child, and when I turned thirty-five, I realized it was now or never. I'd have to take matters into my own hands."

Really, I just got tired of waiting. Sometimes it feels like I've spent my whole life that way, getting more and more frustrated until I finally just did for myself what nobody else would do for me. I was tired of living in a cramped, dingy apartment, so I saved up for a freshly built condo. Tired of busting my ass for a promotion that was always "Oh, it's not in the budget right now, maybe next year," so I quit my job as a supermarket-chain book buyer and opened the Lit Apothecary. Tired of fifteen years of serial monogamy, dating my way through what felt like every man in the city, sniffing and digging like a bloodhound for husband material, so I bought myself a top-of-the-line battery-operated boyfriend.

Going to a fertility clinic is just more of the same pattern. I realized all along that I needed one thing from a man—just one thing—since I wasn't able to find someone I could see myself starting a family with, and the sperm bank was the solution.

"If this doesn't work, I'll adopt. I'm trying IUI first because adoption is expensive, and it can take a while. But I'll make it happen one way or another, whatever it takes."

"IUI?" he asks.

"Sorry. Intrauterine insemination."

Emmett nods slowly, a sober expression on his face. His gaze is intense. "I can't remember the last time I met a woman like you," he murmurs in a low voice with a heat that sinks into my skin. "I would love to help . . . if you've decided to let me."

Down, girl. "I'm glad to hear that."

"And I'd just be the donor. As I've said before, I

don't want any involvement."

I nod. "I've thought a lot about this over the past couple days, and I've decided, yes, I'm interested. Assuming you don't have any diseases or genetic problems." I pull a small plastic cup out of my purse and set it on the table between us.

Emmett blinks at the cup in confusion for a moment. Then his jaw drops and his eyes widen as his stare snaps back up to me. "What the hell is this?"

"I'm not sure a physical relationship is the best idea. Dinner was great, don't get me wrong, but I just don't think sleeping together is a good idea." I nudge the cup a little closer to him with a demure smile. "This is for your sample."

Chapter Four

Emmett

For a moment, all I can do is stare openmouthed at Jenna. Did she just say my *sample*? No way. A fucking pee cup to catch the goods—is she insane?

~~I shouldn't be pissed.~~ She's not exactly asking me for a hardship here. But orgasming into a cup isn't what I want. *She* is, and right up until five seconds ago, I thought we were on the same page about this arrangement. I've been looking forward to taking this sexy firecracker of a woman to my bed tonight, not handing her my jizz in a sterile plastic cup. What a fucking letdown.

"Is there a problem?" she asks, blinking at me.

I manage to unfreeze my brain enough to respond. Leaning closer, I say quietly, "Hell yes, there is. I'm not jacking off into some cup for you in the bathroom of a Mexican restaurant. What did you think I meant by doing this 'the old-fashioned way?' I wasn't talking about using a butter churn."

"Of course I knew you were talking about having sex. I'm not that naive. And I didn't intend for you to do it *here*," she says, and it might be my imagination, but I think I see her flush a little. "I just decided the physical act of making a baby wouldn't work for me."

"Why not?" Could I have misread her that badly? No way. If I know anything, it's how to tell whether a woman is interested in me, and Jenna's been showing all the signs since the moment we met in that elevator.

"Because I didn't want to invite any ... complications." She hesitates. "Look, don't take this the wrong way, you seem great and all, but I barely know you. We met two days ago. We've had one dinner together. I spend more time deciding on my next shoe purchase than the amount of time we've spent together."

Is that all? So she's not the type to fuck on the first date, no big deal. Was she worried about me trying to rush her? I would never pull a dick move like that—but then again, like she just pointed out, she doesn't know me well enough to know that. I have to earn her trust the hard way.

I give her a reassuring smile. "That's an easy problem to fix. We can keep going out and take things as slow as you need."

"But I don't want to take it slow."

My eyebrows dart up. "Oh? I can do quick too."

Her gaze drops for a second and she stammers, "Th-that's not what I meant. I do feel like we click, but I just don't have the time or energy for anything *involved*."

Oh, I get it now. Looks like we're in the same boat when it comes to dating.

I steeple my fingers in front of my chin. "I see where you're coming from. But sex doesn't have to complicate things." In fact, in my experience, sometimes it makes them wonderfully simple. "If you just want to be fuck-buddies, that's fine with me." I flash her a wolfish grin. "More than fine, actually."

Her eyes remain rock steady, unmoved by my flirting. This is the kind of stare down I've given to doomed opponents at the negotiation table, and I always win. But something about Jenna's confidence leaves me feeling unsure.

Breathing a labored sigh, she explains, "This little cup

ensures we avoid falling into any kind of relationship in the first place. I already have a life plan all worked out, and it doesn't include a man."

"Then it's lucky I never have relationships anyway." When she blinks owlishly, I elaborate. "Let me lay it all out for you. You're clearly a very busy woman, and I'm a very busy man. I'm married to my job. It might not be the happiest marriage, but it's still mine, and I don't do infidelity. My life has no room for anything beyond one-night stands. I haven't had a steady girlfriend in almost a decade. Shit, I barely have time to grab a beer with my best friend once a week, let alone take care of a kid. So, if all you want is for me to knock you up and then get the hell out of your life, that works perfectly for me."

"Yeah, that's all I want, no strings and things done on my terms ... before and after, if you get my drift. What if you change your mind, though?" She crosses her arms over her chest. "I don't want to worry about that possibility. Part of the reason I went for a sperm bank is so some stranger wouldn't come crawling out of the woodwork someday, demanding paternity rights."

"I swear, this kid will be one hundred percent yours.

I'm willing to put that promise in writing, if you want. I won't get involved or even have any opinions on how you raise him or her. Trust me, I'm happy to do nothing more than lend a helping dick." *Very, very happy.*

Jenna's expression changes from stubborn to thoughtful. She chews her lower lip, then replies slowly, "Well, if it's legally binding, maybe. And I've heard that orgasms facilitate sperm uptake, so I guess having sex instead of artificial insemination might not hurt my chances of fertilization."

This is the strangest dirty talk I've ever heard, but I'll take my victories however I can get them. She's willing to consider the idea—or at least stop shoving that damn cup at me.

I take the opportunity to press my point further. "Using a sperm sample defeats the whole purpose of my offer anyway. The reason I suggested this in the first place is so you didn't have to resort to . . . what was it you said they did? Getting your cervix catheterized in some cold clinic." I grimace and can't help but notice the way Jenna's mouth has turned down too.

"That's a fair point." She shrugs. "And you're certain

you can be no-strings about this?"

I nod. "Absolutely. You'll be free to go your own way. Hell, if the kid wants to hop a train and run away to join the circus, they can be my guest. Just as long as you never let them go vegan."

She snorts, trying not to smile. "You said you wouldn't have any opinions."

I put up my hands in mock defeat. "Fine. Just put the cup away, for God's sake."

She sighs but tucks it back into her purse, and I'm glad to see it go. Then she adds, "There is one more issue we should talk about."

"Lay it on me." Whatever it is, I'm sure I can deal with it.

"This might not be a once-and-done thing. We might have to keep trying to conceive for months. And since we'd be having unprotected sex, I'd need to see a copy of your test results to be sure you have a clean bill of health, and you'd have to agree to only sleep with me until we're done." Her eyes are sharp, evaluating me, but there's vulnerability in them too. A hint of trepidation as she waits to see how I'll react. "Can you commit to those conditions?"

I should be freaking out. Sleeping with only one woman for however long it takes her to pass a pregnancy test? She's essentially asking me for monogamy until further notice.

But strangely enough, I realize I'm far from turned off. And it's not just because of her assurances that she won't get attached. I can already tell that having her once won't be nearly enough to work her out of my system. Her sexy curves, her smart mouth . . . nope, Jenna isn't a one-night kind of lady.

Intrigued, I nod. "Yeah, I'm still on board. That makes sense, and I'm happy to swap test results." In fact, I'm so on board for that, it's all I can do not to pull her on top of me right now.

"Are you sure you're good with all that?" she asks.

"Absolutely. We're going to fuck, Jenna, and we're going to do it until the job gets done." I stand up, pull out my wallet, and drop a fifty on the table to cover our meal and tip. "So, are you ready to get out of here? No time like the present."

She blinks up at me, looking confused, then chuckles. "Oh no, we're not doing it tonight."

"But you just said—"

"I'm not ovulating yet." She stands up and pats my cheek, her coy smile maddening. "Good night, big boy. Let's talk next Tuesday."

I'm left standing openmouthed on the restaurant patio with tented pants, hot all over, watching her strut away down the street. And not even a good-night kiss to show for it.

Fuck!

• • •

My erection still hasn't died all the way down by the time I get home. I park in the building's basement garage and hurry up to my penthouse, eager for privacy. I can still feel the ghost of Jenna's fingertips brushing my cheek, like the lingering heat of an ember.

I would have expected all this talk of babies and

clinical stuff like ovulation to kill my boner, but somehow, with Jenna, it's the total opposite—sexy as all hell. She puts everything out there so freely, no beating around the bush or getting embarrassed. My usual playmates like to have fun, don't get me wrong, but sometimes it's clear they lack the confidence and directness of maturity. Jenna is completely different. Not a girl, all woman.

God, I can't wait . . .

After draping my sport coat over the back of the couch, I head to my bedroom and sit on the edge of the mattress as I unzip my pants and pull out my stiff cock. A sigh of relief escapes me at the first firm stroke. I close my eyes and let my legs splay open as I focus on the sensations. I jerk myself to dirty thoughts of Jenna, already feeling a warm tingle spreading through my veins.

The fact that she's making me wait to take her just gets me even hotter. What will I do with her when I finally get my hands on her luscious body?

I tighten my grip on my cock and let my imagination run wild with pornographic images. How will she look, sound, smell, feel? Is she a screamer or will I have to pull the noises out of her, overwhelm her before I get to hear her cry out in pleasure? What are her favorite positions? Does she like being pinned, or will she take the reins and straddle me? Whatever she's game for, I'm ready to play.

I pump fast and rough, twisting my fist around the precum-slicked head, rubbing my thumb against the sensitive slit. I picture Jenna everywhere. Writhing on her back underneath me, riding me hard like a rodeo bull, on all fours and pushing her ass back against my hips as I thrust from behind. And I try to imagine what it'll be like to fuck her bare, to feel every bit of her hot, wet pussy clenching around my cock with no condom between us. What it'll be like to empty myself inside her. To make a baby.

This will be a first for me—actively trying to impregnate a woman—and after decades of preventing that from happening, I should feel turned off. Instead, the thought has the opposite effect.

My thighs tremble with my oncoming orgasm. I buck faster and faster, thrusting up into my hand. There's no one here to hear me, no need to restrain myself, so I tip my head back and let out a long, loud groan as thick cum spurts over my fingers.

I slow to a stop, breathing hard. Then I get up to throw my soiled shirt and chinos into the laundry and take a shower before bed. Despite the long day I've had, thoughts of Jenna run rampant through my mind and I'm already feeling the urge to jerk off again.

Next Tuesday, she said.

Jesus. It's only six more days, but it already feels like forever.

Chapter Five

Jenna

It's a typical Tuesday afternoon at the Lit Apothecary. The (deserted) sales floor has been swept, dusted, and polished, the (sparse) gaps on the shelves filled, the (dismal) account ledgers balanced. Britt works on inventorying the back stock while I sort through today's batch of mail in my office. This chore is always an exercise in boredom with the occasional sprinkle of frustration, which is why I put it off until late in the day.

Junk, junk, more junk. Publisher's advance list—I'll set that aside for buying season, if we make it to the next one. And . . . a letter from the chain bookstore who wants to buy us out.

Fucking again? I treat that last one to a death glare and spike it into the trash can without even opening it. It's almost certainly yet another buyout offer, and I have zero patience for any more of their lowball attempts.

My already strained mood threatens to crack when I see the return address on the next envelope. I slit it open and my fears are confirmed. It's a snotty warning from the property management company who handles our storefront, demanding our rent. That's the third bill due this week ... and the third we'll have to beg for an extension on.

Groaning to myself, I mutter, "Goddamn it!"

I tried to be quiet, but evidently Britt still heard me from the stockroom. She pokes her blond head around the doorjamb. "You okay, Jenna?"

"There's no blood or broken bones, if that's what you mean." I sigh, holding up the offending piece of paper pinched between my thumb and finger, as if I'm showing her a dead rat.

Britt may be ten years younger than me and my only employee, but she's been here since the very first day I opened the Lit Apothecary. Every struggle and accidentally shouted swear word, all my bad days, she's been privy to them.

"Sorry. I'm just a little stressed out."

Britt touches my shoulder. "It's cool, I know. I'm sure you'll figure something out," she says softly.

Will I, though? I bite my tongue to avoid infecting her with any more of my growing pessimism. I gave myself two years to make this business work, and it's been twenty-three months. I promised myself I wouldn't dip into my savings to keep it afloat—promised that I would make it succeed of its own accord. Only now, that doesn't seem very likely.

The only option I can come up with is one I don't want to think about. When I quit my old job as a book buyer, my boss told me I could come back anytime. But, dammit, the Lit Apothecary is my baby, my pet project, my dream. I've invested so much in this . . . I don't want to fail at it. I don't want to go back to corporate life with a manager riding my ass all the time. Yet here I am, on the verge of throwing in the towel, with no idea how to avoid that humbling last resort.

Finally, I just say, "I hope so, Britt. I hope so."

The sober moment is interrupted by loud ringing. *Emmett?* The thought leaps into my mind of its own accord. But when I check my phone, I see it's not a call, it's the alarm I set to remind me of my doctor's appointment in half an hour. Huh . . . I got so wrapped up in stressing out over our finances, I didn't even notice the workday was over. I guess time flies when you're having an aneurysm.

I shoot Britt an apologetic look. "Sorry, I have to run. Can you handle—"

"Of course. You already told me this morning you needed to leave early," she says, smiling. "I still don't get why you're so into this whole baby thing when you could have any man at your beck and call, but hey, you do you. Go ahead and get going. I'll close up shop in a bit."

"Thanks," I shout as I rush out the door.

I'm so keyed up, it takes an effort to stay at the speed limit as I drive to the doctor's office. I've been looking forward to this visit for the past week. Even though my bookshop may be in the toilet, at least my plans for motherhood are right on track, and that cheers me up immensely.

The prospect of making progress toward a baby turns my thoughts to Emmett, which only improves my mood more. I had a great time with him last week. Everything about him is a breath of fresh air. He's smart but not arrogant about it, considerate but not a pushover, bold and direct but not rude or presumptuous. He knows what he wants and he pursues it. He doesn't play games or feed a girl lines. I like that he's older, and he doesn't want kids himself. Not to mention he's sexy as sin.

Most importantly, something about him just ... inspires trust. At first, I assumed he'd flake out on me, but our dinner together proved me wrong about his reliability. I really got the sense that I can count on him to follow through on his promises. I was so convinced that he meant what he said and that I wouldn't need a sperm bank, that I called to schedule my appointment first thing the very next morning. Luckily, they were able to squeeze me in that day, and I snagged the first step in my treatment—a prescription for a hormone pill that I'll need to take daily, which Dr. Kaur said would get my cycle on a predictable schedule and release my eggs like clockwork.

I perch restlessly on a bench in the lobby, practically vibrating with eagerness until the nurse calls me back to an exam room. As she takes my temperature and blood pressure, she smiles at me, as if she can tell how close to exploding I feel.

Soon Dr. Kaur, a tiny, matronly Indian woman and my trusted ob-gyn, swishes in with a brisk flap of her white coat and plops down at her computer desk.

"Hello again, Miss Porter. Let me just pull up the nurse's notes here . . ." She clicks around for a minute. "Yes, your bloodwork and ultrasound results have all been very promising. Hormone levels are on target. How are you doing with the hormone? Any hot flashes, fatigue, joint pain, headaches?"

I shake my head at each item in her rapid-fire litany of side effects. "Maybe I've been a little tired, but not enough to warrant any concern, I don't think."

"Excellent. Clearly, this drug is a good fit for you." She types in a few comments, purses her lips, and nods. "I think we're ready to go."

I cheer silently. "Great. What are the next steps?"

She peers through her thick glasses at the medical chart on the screen. "Your insemination method . . . last time you were here, in the notes it says you've changed your mind about artificial insemination and you want to use scheduled intercourse instead. That's still your plan?"

"Yes." Hopefully she doesn't ask too many questions about where exactly I'm getting the goods. All she needs to know is I've locked down my own personal supply of fresh sperm. The fact that it comes in such attractive packaging is just a nice bonus.

"All right, I only wanted to confirm." Dr. Kaur scribbles on a notepad, tears off the top sheet, and swivels her chair around to hand it to me. "I'm giving you a prescription for an injectable, also known as a 'trigger shot.' This will induce ovulation. Fill it immediately and use it tonight. You'll need to have intercourse at least once a day for the next two to three days—"

"Three days?" I blurt, accidentally interrupting her.

She suppresses a smile. "Yes, starting twenty-four hours after injection."

Twenty-four hours, huh? I nod, already making plans. Looks like I know where I'll be tomorrow night, and the next night, and the night after that. "Okay. And how soon will I know if it worked?"

"You'll take a pregnancy test in two weeks." She opens a drawer and pulls out a business card. "This website will link you to an instructional video for self-administering the injectable."

"O-of course." My heart flutters in combined nervousness and excitement. Imagining what it will feel like to stab myself in the stomach every four weeks makes me slightly queasy, but I still can't wait to get started. After wanting this for so long, it's finally happening.

Soon I'm going to have a baby of my own . . . my own little snuggly bundle of joy to love and spoil and watch grow. The thought makes me feel warm inside, and deepens my resolve about doing this. Even the not-so-fun parts.

Dr. Kaur gives me a small smile and I thank her again, then check out at the front desk and leave with my precious new prescription tucked snugly in my purse.

Walking back across the parking lot, I text Emmett. *What are you doing tomorrow night?*

In a matter of seconds, he replies, *Fucking you, hopefully.*

I freeze in my tracks for a moment. They're only words, three little words on a screen, but I can hear his husky voice saying them in my mind, and a tingle of anticipation shoots straight to the pit of my stomach. Or maybe somewhere farther south, if I'm being completely honest with myself.

A flicker of doubt halts me with my hand on my car door. For a second, I wonder whether this decision is really a good idea, or if my libido has led me astray. The kind of butterflies Emmett gives me are way out of proportion to what we're doing here. Our arrangement is supposed to be about sperm, eggs, and ovulation cycles, not lust and orgasms. *I'm in this to get pregnant. That's it.*

On the other hand ... *fuck it*. I deserve a little fun once in a while. I get into my car, shut the door, and text him back with jittery hands: *Okay, your place or mine?*

His response comes quickly. *You get right to the point, don't you? How about dinner first?*

I hesitate again. Dinner last week was nice, but maybe it was also a mistake. We're not dating. Emmett isn't my boyfriend. I should put the brakes on this relationship before it becomes anything more than a business transaction.

No thanks, I don't think we should, I finally reply.

Come on, we gotta eat sometime. Can I tempt you with Los Platitos?

I frown down at my phone. Well, shit. Now the jerk is just playing dirty. I'm even weaker for tapas than I am for Mexican food, and that restaurant is my all-time favorite. How the hell does he know that? Or maybe we just have that in common.

My resolve wavers, then crumbles. *Fine, you win. I'll meet you there at six.*

I pocket my phone and drive away, first to the pharmacy, then home. I can already tell I'll have a hard time getting to sleep tonight . . . for a lot of reasons.

Chapter Six

Emmett

I click my phone off, smiling triumphantly at how I coaxed Jenna into dinner, and finish wrapping up the day's work. My good mood is even better because my best friend and I finally settled on plans to grab a drink tonight. Between my insane hours and Jesse trying to juggle work with family, we haven't met up in a couple of weeks, and I'll be damned if I'm going to be late.

I drive to Nealy's Bar, park at the curb, and stroll into the underlit den of neon with its peeling varnish and lingering scent of tobacco. This place is a first-degree shithole, but it's also one of our old college hangouts, so even though we both can afford much better now, we still visit from time to time for sentimental reasons.

I walk over to where Jesse is already sitting at the sticky bar and clap him on the shoulder. "Hey, glad I could drag you out."

Jesse swivels around on his stool with a wide grin. "It's been too long, man. I almost forgot what you look like."

I pull out my wallet and reach past Jesse to slap my credit card on the counter, which gets the bartender's attention. "I'm here now and you're stuck with me, so let's drink."

We order and pay at the bar, grab our cheap domestic brews, and head to a corner table where we can hear ourselves think over the jukebox wailing country music.

Jesse takes a long drink and smiles as he sets the

bottle down. "Damn, that's good. I mean, I know it's practically horse piss, but somehow it tastes so much better when you're out of the house, right?"

"Well, it's sure not the company," I say, taking a slug of my own beer.

"Fuck you," Jesse says with a smile. "So, how's the high-powered bachelor lifestyle?"

I snort. "Like a tax attorney doesn't know how it feels to have money."

"That's not what I meant and you know it. Come on," he says, "let a poor family man live vicariously through you. Who's the flavor of the month this time?"

This ribbing is a game as old as Jesse's marriage. He likes to joke about how my life must be so easy and fun, just one big party, but I've seen how he worships the ground his wife and kids walk on.

"We both know damn well you'd never trade places with me."

He shrugs. "Who says I want to? All I'm asking for is a quick peek at the sweet life. And the only thing I like more than a good dirty story is annoying you."

I play along by heaving an exaggerated sigh of annoyance. "Well, if you insist, but it's just the usual debauchery. Fast cars, fast women, snorting coke off the copy machine, keg stands on the conference table."

That gets a laugh out of him. "You're right, I shouldn't have asked. Falling asleep here."

I chuckle, dropping the fake tone. "Really, it's been the same old grind. I'm still up to my eyeballs in contract negotiations. That little bookstore downtown we're trying to buy still won't give us the time of day. You know, the regular shit I always bore you with." I can't resist adding, "Although I do have a date tomorrow night."

Jesse bounces his eyebrows at me. "A date? I didn't know you still bothered wining and dining women before screwing them. Picking up sorority girls in bars seems more your style."

I chuckle into my beer. "For your information, asshole, I go on real dates all the time. They just don't result in girlfriends."

For a moment, I consider dropping the subject and not revealing anything else. But Jesse is my best friend. I don't like lying to him. Plus, I have to have *someone* to talk to about this, and I know he won't meddle.

As casually as possible, I say, "Actually . . . can you keep a secret?"

"I hope so. Confidentiality is kind of an important part of the whole attorney gig," he replies. "What's on your mind?"

"It's kind of a funny story. So this woman I'm going out with—Jenna's her name—you know how I met her? Last week we got stuck in an elevator together in my building. And I found out she's trying to start a family, so I offered to help her."

Jesse's beer stops halfway to his lips. "Help . . . how?" he says slowly.

"How do you think? You have two kids, dude, I know you know how they're made. You know, the birds and the bees and baby makes three, although this baby is only going to make two."

Staring at me like I just grew another head, Jesse

carefully lowers his glass to the table. "This better be a bad joke." His voice is absolutely flat.

I shake my head. "She wants to have a baby, I happen to own a well-endowed and functioning set of baby-production equipment, so she's going to use me to get pregnant. Simple," I say, then I almost rupture something trying not to laugh at the way Jesse's eyes widen.

"Have you lost your damn mind?" he hisses at me in an undertone like we're discussing state secrets. "What in the actual fuck were you thinking?"

I give him a weird look. "That I would . . . do a lady a favor and get laid at the same time?"

He pinches the bridge of his nose. "Never mind, it doesn't matter. I'm sure your big head wasn't the one doing the thinking anyway. But before your little head goes within a mile of this Jenna woman, you need to have her sign a paternity affidavit, work out custody, get—"

I hold up my hand to shield myself from Jesse's lawyer-mode frenzy. "What? No, dude, you know me. I don't want anything to do with this kid, and she doesn't want that either. It's not going to be a big deal."

"Don't 'dude' me," Jesse huffs. "You're thirty-eight. You might change your mind about settling down."

"And give up all this?" I gesture around us at the dive bar in all its dim, seedy glory.

It was a joke and he knows it, but he gives me a withering look anyway. "Oh yes, of course not. Because the novelty will definitely never, ever wear off of booty calls with twenty-year-olds. Alternating sleeping alone with wondering if you've contracted an STD is so much fun."

I roll my eyes. "That happened *one time*, and the test came out negative."

"Just shut up and listen to me for a second. Whether you want to be a dad or not, you still need paperwork either way, and you need it ASAP. Thank God you said something to me before you fucked her."

"Would you relax?" I snap. His panic is starting to piss me off, especially the way he talks about Jenna. It's like he thinks I can't be trusted—or he thinks *she* can't, despite not knowing the first thing about her. "I have this under control."

He takes a deep breath and lets it whoosh out in a loud sigh. "Okay, okay, I'll try to chill. But, seriously, what if she changes her mind and comes after you later?"

"I'm telling you she won't do that," I grumble. I trust Jenna. She knows what she wants, and it's not my money.

Jesse still looks completely unconvinced, but he nods. "Well, if you're sure this is what you want . . . please let me at least draft some contracts to protect you, just in case. You waive your right to custody, she waives your obligation to provide child support, you both agree to mutual nondisclosure, basic stuff like that. I'll email you everything so you and Jenna can both sign them."

After taking a sip of my beer, I give him a noncommittal grunt. "Send whatever you want. I'll take a look at it if it makes you feel better."

Jesse smirks, knowing he's won. "They'll be in your in-box by noon tomorrow."

I shake my head at him, smiling despite myself. *Stubborn bastard* . . . There's a reason why we've stayed best friends for so many years. "Enough about all that. Tell me what's new with Sheri and the kids."

"Nothing really. It's all good, though. Most nights by the time I get home, it's to catch the tail end of *Finding Nemo* with the kids conked out on the couch, and Sheri almost right behind them. So I bring her a glass of wine and we sit together for a little while before putting everyone to bed."

"Half-asleep wine-drinking watching *Finding Nemo* in a pile of rug rats? How romantic," I say dryly.

Jesse shrugs, grinning. "Parents grab their romance where they can find it."

We chat for a while longer, catching up on work and other topics while eating stale pretzels, and order a second beer. Jesse is my oldest friend in the world, and it's relaxing just being in the company of someone who gets you.

Finally, he drains the last of his beer and stands up. "I should probably get going. Thanks for the beer, man. Let's do this again soon."

I get up to pull him in for a hearty handshake and a

parting pat on the back. "Definitely."

• • •

I didn't take our conversation to heart at first. Whatever he sends me tomorrow, I'll read over and sign. I'm not worried about Jenna wanting anything more from me than what my body can give her. But on the way home, driving alone through dark streets, I start to mull over more deeply how different our lives are.

This isn't the first time talking to Jesse has made me think about family. He complains a lot about being a father—too many responsibilities, not enough quality time with his wife, the shenanigans his kids get into—but I can tell it's all just good-natured bitching. He and Sheri are the picture of wedded bliss, smitten since the day they met, and the only things they love more than each other are their two munchkins.

What Jesse has seems to work well for him. But for me . . .

It would never work. I'm all business, all the time—my job demands everything from me. If I ever did marry, it would end up turning into a rerun of my parents' mistakes. My workaholic, emotionally constipated father left Mom so lonely, she went hunting for affection from any man who'd look twice at her. And when the midlife crisis hit, Dad started having his own affairs too, and eventually traded Mom in for a younger model. It was one big ugly cliché—the CEO fucking his secretary, his wife fucking the pool boy, their three kids left in the lurch—and I don't care to repeat the cycle.

Even if my hypothetical wife didn't mind that I worked all the time and didn't fuck the pool boy, who's to say that we wouldn't just tire of each other. Or fight all the time. Or end up hating each other as much as my parents do. It's just not worth it. I'm not cut out for it.

I would never say this to his face, but deep down, I suspect Jesse and Sheri are a fluke. A freak accident of probability. Ninety-nine times out of a hundred, human hearts aren't strong enough to bear the weight of careers, children, stress, the plain old boring grind of daily life. Love is only a temporary delirium, and sooner or later, reality and its demands will start eating away at the happiness. Cracks will appear and spread in whatever you try to build. And the inevitable collapse of wedded bliss . . . what's the point of doing that to myself? To anyone I care about?

Better not to begin at all. Better, easier, to just stay alone.

The silence of my darkened penthouse greets me. The large, empty space is a little chilly after my long day out. I walk to the hall thermostat, flipping on lights as I go, and turn up the heat. Then I double back to check the fridge. There's no real point in cooking for one, especially not at this hour, when I'm already tired. A quick dinner will do. I grab some bread and cold cuts, nudge the fridge door shut with my foot, and throw together a sandwich.

Then I pause, considering the plate in my hand. The food doesn't look great, to put it mildly. The thought of eating suddenly strikes me as unappealing. *Hmm . . . maybe dredging up old childhood memories made me lose my appetite. Fuck it, I'll just shower and go to sleep.* I put plastic wrap on the plate and stick it in the fridge for later.

I undress and step into the steaming spray with a hiss, then a sigh of pleasure. The scalding water is just the thing to relax me. But rather than calm me down like I planned, it gets my blood pumping, and my thoughts turn toward what I have waiting for me tomorrow night.

Jenna . . .

I'm more than ready for a little time with her. Hell, as long as there's a lot of orgasms, I'm not at all concerned with how long it takes.

My cock twitches with interest. I let my hand drift down, over my chest and abs, following the path of the trickling water. In less than twenty-four hours, Jenna will be the one caressing me like this. Exploring me. And I'll get to do the same to her, map every inch of that incredible body, find out what pleases her best. I'll give her screaming orgasms until she melts into a sweaty, satisfied mess.

I can't fucking wait.

Within a minute, I'm already fully hard, and I stifle a moan at the first stroke. God, I'm so ready for her. What I wouldn't give to have Jenna in the shower with me right now, naked and wet, her curves flushed with heat. I'd press her up against the tile wall and find out what her pussy tastes like . . .

But all that will happen tomorrow, not now. Not yet.

And until then, I shouldn't blow my load early. Biting my lip, I force myself to drop my hand and ignore the ache of frustrated lust in my groin. I want to save it all for her.

As I shampoo my hair, I smirk. One thing I know for sure . . .

I'm going to rock her world tomorrow.

Chapter Seven

Jenna

The next evening, I left work a little early to prepare. I showered, shaved all the vital regions, blow-dried my hair, and am now pacing around my bedroom wrapped in a towel, trying to figure out what to wear. Balance is crucial. I want to look nice but not overdressed, and definitely not too sexy.

I consider my fanciest underthings—a lacy black lingerie set—then pass them over in favor of plain white cotton. Sensible underwear for a sensible night of making a baby.

Just because Emmett is going to see me naked tonight doesn't mean I have to put on a whole song and dance for him. No big deal. He's only the most handsome man I've ever seen, and this will be the first time I've gotten laid in almost a year, and . . .

Oh my God, stop it, woman. Please, just stop thinking and cover your tits.

As I pull on my panties, I'm careful not to brush the small, but sore red welt near my navel. I injected my first hCG trigger shot last night. While it wasn't a barrel of laughs, it also wasn't nearly as bad as my mind had built it up to be. As with most scary things in life, I found that the best approach was to just gather my courage and take the leap fast, before I could psych myself out of it. Now if only I could stop overthinking this date too.

No, no, this is not a date. What's happening tonight is absolutely nothing like a date. It's just ... informal sperm donation.

Oh my God, I'm really doing this, aren't I? Negotiating a stud deal for myself like a horse breeder or something? I stare into my closet like it contains the controls to a jumbo jet instead of the same old wardrobe I should find easy to choose from.

Okay, stop freaking out. Think of it like a business meeting. Just because it's for knocking me up doesn't make the rules of engagement any different. Insert penis A into slot B. We stay professional, because anything more will just confuse my heart and blur the lines, and I can't let that happen.

Sure, Emmett is attractive and funny and kind, and

that's a big part of why I chose him ... but not in a boyfriend kind of way. This isn't a romantic audition. It's just because his traits are good enough that I'd want them passed on to my child, that's all. Besides, it's no shame to pick a high-quality partner who also happens to be so good looking it hurts. I might as well have fun while I'm working on getting fertilized.

Yep, totally cool and rational, no complicated feelings allowed. And if he does or says one single thing that makes me uncomfortable, I'm not above telling him to get out of my bedroom and go jack off in that cup. I have a whole binder full of men I could pick from at the sperm bank.

While I'm thinking about it, I grab the plastic specimen jar and toss it in my purse, just in case. In the process, I catch a glimpse at the clock and almost panic because, holy shit, it's already 5:15. How was I dithering around in my underwear for half an hour?

No more nonsense. I need laser focus. I need to just fucking pick an outfit already.

I go back to the closet. A mulberry peasant blouse, fawn-colored suede ankle boots, and my most flattering pair of dark jeans—sure, that's fine. I dress as fast as I can while still avoiding the sore spot on my stomach. For a moment, I fret over the question of jewelry, makeup, and perfume, then say out loud, "Oh, for God's sake, what I wore to work is fine," and restrain myself to the minimum. Then I'm out the door and on my way to Los Platitos.

Like he did at our last dinner meeting, Emmett is waiting for me outside, looking nothing short of dashing. He flashes me a brilliant smile. "Hey there, beautiful. You hungry?"

The innocent question seems a lot dirtier coming from his full lips. And it's disarming how he always seems so pleased to see me.

"Starving," I say truthfully.

We walk together into the warm ambience of Los Platitos, with its amber lighting, dark wood decor, and rich scents of saffron, garlic, and smoke. Even though I only live a couple of blocks away, I haven't visited in a long time. It's pretty pricey, and it moved well out of my budget when I opened the Lit Apothecary.

The hostess seats us at a small round table, and a waitress soon appears. "Good evening," she chirps. "Can I get you two something to drink?"

"I'll have iced tea," I reply.

"I'll have a gin and tonic, pl—" Emmett starts to say, but I quickly interrupt him.

"No. Sorry, he'll have tonic water with lime."

He blinks, and the waitress's brow furrows slightly.

When I realize how rude that sounded, I turn to Emmett. "Remember . . . uh, dear, you're not supposed to have alcohol."

He still looks confused but plays along and nods at the waitress. "Right. My mistake; I forgot. She's right."

Her expression softens into a smile, as if she finds us endearing. "A close call. All right, one iced tea and one tonic water with lime. I'll get those drinks right out to you."

As soon as the waitress is gone, Emmett asks me, "I'm sorry, but since when do I not drink? I'm sure that waitress thinks I'm on my way to an AA meeting as soon as we finish eating."

I offer him an apologetic smile. "Sorry. It's just that I want your swimmers to be in top shape tonight."

He nods slowly, understanding. "Ah. Well, I promise they are . . . dear."

I answer his teasing smirk by rolling my eyes. "Don't make fun of me. Would you rather I'd told her the whole story?" Feigning affectionate concern was the easiest way over that little speed bump.

"Fine, I'll lay off. So, how was your day?" he asks, sounding genuinely interested.

I shrug a little. "Eh, it was okay. I don't really feel like talking about work." *On dates*, I stop myself from finishing.

"Fair enough. I don't either." He leans back in his chair and it creaks. "How about . . . do you have any hobbies?"

"Mostly I just read." Alone in bed at night, sipping a glass of wine. All I need to complete the cozy-but-kind-of-sad picture is a cat on my lap.

"Nice. I wish I had more time to read, myself." The corners of his eyes crinkle. "Or maybe I do have the time and I just waste it on TV. What's your favorite book?"

"You're making me choose?" I widen my eyes, pretending to be scandalized. "How could you ever do that to a poor bibliophile?"

He laughs. "Okay, jeez. Can I ask your favorite genre, at least? Mine is crime fiction, if you want to know."

I shouldn't want to know. We're not here to get close. We're here to eat and hash out the final details of getting a bun in my oven. But even knowing that, I find myself suddenly reluctant to shatter the casual mood. Besides, I love talking about books.

There isn't any harm in it, is there? We can just enjoy a night out at a nice restaurant right now and save the heavy stuff for later.

I ponder his question. "I like mysteries too. I'm pretty omnivorous when it comes to books. But I think, if I absolutely had to pick . . . ugh, this is so hard. Let's say satire, gothic romance, and postmodern literature are somewhere in my top five. Oh, and historical nonfiction."

We're briefly interrupted by the waitress returning with our drinks. We thank her and order half a dozen different tapas plates.

Emmett sips his lime tonic water. "Hmm ... this actually isn't half bad. Anyway, that's quite a list. I'm going to guess you were an English major?"

"Classics and philosophy, actually," I reply, stirring sugar into my iced tea. "But I might have added English too if I'd had more time." Raising me alone, Mom couldn't afford to contribute much to my college fund, and my scholarships came with a graduation deadline. I was lucky for the four years I got.

Emmett hums appreciatively. "Damn, woman, now I feel out of my league. Did you learn to speak Latin?"

I make an uncertain noise. "I took some basic language classes, but my emphasis was more on art, literature, and history, and I'm sure I've lost it all by now anyway."

"Come on, give it a try," he says. "Talk nerdy to me."

Our food arrives and I pop a bacon-wrapped fig into

my mouth while I try to think back almost fifteen years. *Hmm . . . there's one quote that should definitely get a laugh out of him, if I can only remember it.*

"Well," I say finally, "I might still know part of a poem by Catullus. I memorized it in college because I thought it'd make a funny party trick." He'll see why in a minute.

Haltingly, I start to recite it in all its indecipherable glory. Normally, I'd feel self-conscious reciting a poem in Latin in front of anyone after all these years, but it feels fun.

Emmett raises his eyebrows, impressed. "Wow. What does that mean?"

I try to keep a straight face as I translate, "I will fuck you in the ass and mouth—"

I can't even get through the first line before Emmett interrupts me by cracking up. "What . . . ha-ha . . . what the hell? So you *do* have a dirty mind."

"It's more a pissed-off poem than a dirty one. But I never claimed my mind was one hundred percent clean," I retort playfully. "I just don't advertise dirtiness like you do."

Then I hesitate. Wait, no, this is way too close to flirting. I should pull back and move to a serious topic.

I fiddle with my napkin in my lap. "Not to kill the mood or anything, but we should talk about ... what we're doing later."

His smile turns devilish. "Oh? I think that's the opposite of killing the mood."

I ignore the heat that climbs into my cheeks. "Before we have sex, I need to know for sure that you'll never try to get involved. I want to raise my child my way—alone. No co-parenting, not even any shared holidays, nada. This is my plan, and if you can't agree to that—no offense, but I'll just go back to the sperm bank."

Emmett's eyebrow quirks. "Haven't we already talked about this?"

"Yes, but I wanted to give you one last chance to back out." I raise my brows urgently, looking him square in the eye. "So if you need to think it over a little longer . . ."

"You've got nothing to worry about," he says. I expected him to be annoyed by my interrogation, but his tone is only reassuring, and maybe a little amused. "My answer hasn't changed since last week. Trust me . . . as a busy executive, I have no interest in midnight feedings and diaper patrol. That stuff is all you."

I nod, slightly calmed. "Good, so we're in agreement."

Instead of changing the subject to something more fun, Emmett considers me for a moment, then sighs thoughtfully. "Listen . . . I hope you trust me, and I know I trust you, but if it helps ease your mind, my attorney friend drafted some contracts. Practically shoved them down my throat, in fact. You want to look them over now?"

"Really?" I blink. "Um . . . yeah, actually, I would like that."

He pulls out his phone and forwards me an email with three attachments. I read while eating, my phone in one hand and a piece of foie-gras toast in the other. Emmett says nothing, patiently letting me concentrate. I feel a little bad for ignoring him . . . but then again, I remind myself, we're having a business meeting, not a date. Discussing this agreement is the entire point of us coming here.

I notice Emmett's already signed the documents: Jonathan Emmett Smith II. Huh, I guess he goes by his middle name. I guess I don't blame a man called "the Second" for wanting to differentiate himself from his father. Something seems familiar about his name, but it's not like Smith is an uncommon name. Whatever, I'm probably just remembering an old coworker or something. I focus on the contract language itself.

Years working in business has given me a talent for speed-reading legalese. Finally, I put away my phone and nod at him. "These look pretty solid. I'll add my signature tomorrow and send them back to you."

He cocks his head. "Tomorrow? Not before you let me into your bedroom?"

I lean my chin on my hand. "Nah. I think . . . I trust you too. At least enough to wait until the morning after."

A slow but dazzling grin spreads over his handsome features. "Glad to hear it. Now, let's dig in. This meal looks incredible."

We enjoy a wonderful dinner together, chatting about food, books, the hassles and rewards of managing a business, and all the other interests we're slowly discovering we have in common. We splurge on lemon-ginger tartlet for dessert. When the bill arrives, Emmett insists on paying, and I can't find it in me to put up too much of a fight.

He signs the receipt, adding a generous tip. Then he pushes his chair out and extends his hand to me. "Shall we?"

I swallow. Only one more event remains in the evening, and there's a sensual smolder in his eyes. An unmistakable promise of pleasure.

I almost take his hand. Instead, I stand up on my own. "Y-yeah, let's go. My place is just a short walk away."

"Really? So is mine. I guess we live only a few blocks apart."

Close. Too close. Our shoulders bump as we exit into the cool night air and make our way toward my place

. . . and my bed.

Chapter Eight

Emmett

With my hand lightly touching the small of her back, I follow Jenna's lead into her building, up two flights of stairs, and down a hall until she stops in front of a door.

"Here we are." She unlocks it and pushes it open. "Sorry it's kind of a mess," she says as she flicks on the light. "I've been crazy busy."

I glance around her living room with curiosity. The plush green couch looks like it could swallow people whole, and it's strewn with throw blankets and pillows in jewel tones and bohemian patterns. Framed landscape panoramas and art nouveau prints hang on the walls. And of course, a large bookcase dominates the far side of the room, overflowing with books of all shapes, sizes, and jacket colors.

Overall, the eclectic decor isn't necessarily what I would have guessed, but it suits Jenna. I can see why she likes it. Cozy, soft, inviting . . . I might even use the word *cute*. It's a far cry from the sleek, hypermodern aesthetic of my penthouse. Compared to this, my place feels uncomfortably sterile instead of elegant.

"I don't see any mess," I reply truthfully. Sure, there's some clutter, but it makes the place feel lived-in. Like somewhere people go to feel at home, not just to sleep.

She chuckles. "That's nice of you to say. Do you want anything to drink?" She bends down to slide off her boots and drops them in the tray by the entry closet.

"No thanks." I start to take off my shoes too, and am struck with sudden nerves.

This is it, I think, my heart rate picking up. When we first met, I wondered how Jenna was still single, and now that we've gotten to know each other better, I still have no fucking idea. She seems like the total package—not just gorgeous but smart, funny, and cool. Utterly magnetic. And after all our talking about sex, I'm finally getting my hands on her, getting inside her. I've been half-hard since last night from anticipation alone.

For the first time since high school, I feel unsure of myself. This isn't exactly a conventional post-date scenario. How should I initiate? Are we going to ease into intimacy, maybe sit on the couch and talk first? Or will we just cut to the chase and hop right into bed?

"Okay, then." Jenna takes a few steps across the living room, then pauses to glance back at me. "Are you ready now?"

That answers my question. If she wants to get straight to the main event, I'm not complaining. "Absolutely," I reply with a grin.

We continue through the hall and into the bedroom. But instead of turning on the light, the shadow beside me that is Jenna moves around in the dark. I hear fabric rustling—she's getting undressed? *What the hell?* I frown in disappointment. I wanted to see all of her, and I never would have pegged her as the shy type.

I feel the wall for the light switch, find none, and grope around blindly. Jenna steps away. Bedsprings creak, followed by more rustling. My hand hits a lamp and I click it on.

Jenna is in bed, lying on her back under the sheets, not even looking at me.

"What are you doing?" I ask, trying not to sound exasperated.

All she says is, "Come on. Turn that off and get in."

Starting to get annoyed, I click the bedside lamp back off and strip as fast as I can, dropping my clothes on the floor since I can't fucking see to put them anywhere else.

A second later, her voice in the darkness asks, "Are you coming?"

"Hold on, I'm taking off my clothes," I mutter, concentrating on trying not to stumble.

"Why?" She sounds like she genuinely has no idea.

"What do you mean, why?" I'm totally bewildered. "We're having sex. I'm getting naked. Isn't that normal?"

"I'm well aware we're having sex," she says with a slightly frosty tone. "What I meant was, you don't have to remove everything, you know?"

I'm torn between laughing and getting pissed. This whole situation is spiraling into insanity. I wasn't prepared for any of this. "Because I want to," I say flatly. "Is it a problem if I'm naked?"

A pause, then she says, "I guess not, but, I mean . . . you don't need to be."

I don't know how to respond to that, so I just climb into bed beside her. My body warms in anticipation—finally, I'm going to touch her. Inhaling her wonderful flowery fragrance, I lean close for our first-ever kiss. But I pull right back when she stiffens at the touch of my lips.

"Are you okay?" I ask.

"Y-yeah, I'm fine," she stammers. "I wasn't expecting it, that's all."

Is she nervous? As gently as I can, I say, "Do you need a rain check? We can try again some other time."

"No," she says, and the sudden fierceness in her voice makes me blink. "I want you to fuck me."

"All right," I say slowly, confused. If she's not getting cold feet, then what's the problem? "I can do that. But is it all right if we kiss first?"

Another long pause. "I . . . guess so."

I lean forward again. I try to ease her into the idea of

my lips on hers, deciding to go slow, keep it chaste, no tongue. The awkwardness gradually melts out of her body and her lips start to open against mine, at first just accepting me, then reciprocating.

Despite everything she's done to throw me off, I start to get back into the groove. I pull her close. But when our bodies brush together, instead of warm, velvety skin against my bare chest, I feel cotton.

Jesus, Mary, and Joseph. She's still wearing her bra.

I skim my hand down over the delightfully round curve of her hip and feel a waistband. She's still wearing panties too. No wonder I'm thinking about Jesus, Mary, and Joseph, because apparently Jenna's relying on immaculate conception to get pregnant.

Weird. She took off her clothes, but not her underwear? I guess we're still in the foreplay stage, though, so I can work with this.

I cup her crotch and grin against her mouth when she squeaks. My fingers stroke through the thin fabric, teasing her. I'll work her up a little before I move on to grinding the heel of my hand against her clit—

But I never get to that part because Jenna freezes up again, and I pull my hand away.

I draw back and break the kiss, ignoring her tiny questioning murmur. "Okay, what's going on with you? Are you feeling all right? Should we stop?"

"I can take them off." She wriggles around under the covers. "There, all ready for you."

"No, not all ready," I huff. "The panties aren't the point. You're probably not even wet yet."

"I have lube."

She rolls away. I hear the scrape of a wooden drawer, then rummaging.

It finally dawns on me. She's expecting me to just stick it to her. Get in and get out. Use her like nothing more than a warm hole. Wham, bam, thank you, ma'am. Deposit my semen and move on.

Well, no fucking thank you. I might as well be jacking off into that damn plastic cup. I'm not going to fuck somebody who lies limp like a dead fish … the thought makes my skin crawl. I jump out of bed and flip on the lamp.

Jenna sits up to squint at me in the sudden flood of light. "What's wrong?"

"What *isn't* wrong?" I snap. I start pacing around the bedroom, too angry to care that I'm buck naked and probably look ridiculous. "I didn't sign up for a pump-and-dump. And I'm sorry, but this isn't what I expected, not what we talked about." I turn at the end of the bedroom and make a second lap around the room, my brain still processing. "I have some rules of my own. First, we're going to have foreplay. Second, I'm going to make you come for me, more than once."

She doesn't answer, and I turn back to her. Her eyes are wide and she's blinking at me, apparently stunned.

Then I realize where she's looking, and despite my anger, I have to smirk. Annoyance and confusion have dampened my lust, but I know I still measure up, even with a slightly wilted erection. "Like what you see?" I tease. "It gets even bigger, I promise."

"Wh-what?" Her eyes snap up to mine. I note with amusement that her cheeks are flushed. "Uh . . . it'll do just fine."

Smugly, I cross my arms over my chest, making a point of not covering my lower half. "Of course it will. Did you hear a word I said?"

She stares steadily at me. "Yeah, you want me to come. That's fine. The vaginal contractions of orgasm increase the chance of concept—"

Interrupting her with my sexual frustration, I growl, "But how am I supposed to do that if you'll barely let me touch you?"

"Oh, you don't have to worry about it. I just figured I'd use my vibrator after you left," she says nonchalantly.

My jaw drops and I gape at her. "What the fuck kind of men have you been with?" *Obviously, the kind who don't know how to use their dick.* "Never mind—that changes now. We need to talk." I sit on the wooden chair in front of her desk, ignoring the unpleasant chill on my bare ass.

She sits up, tugging the sheet up to cover her bra. "Talk about what?" Now she's getting annoyed too, but I don't really feel bad about it. "You took high-school sex ed, right? All you have to do is come inside me."

"Trust me, I know all about the birds and the bees. But I want you to enjoy this too, not just put up with it for the sake of getting pregnant." I look in her eyes, hoping she can hear my sincerity. "I want to fuck *you*, Jenna Porter, the whole woman, not just . . . leave my sample at the door and walk away." I grimace. "So, can we try that?" *Actually having fun in bed like normal, horny people*, I don't add.

"Hmm . . ." She chews her lip, as if the idea of enjoying sex is brand new to her and she has to mull it over.

I don't understand why this is apparently such a hard decision, but I try to sit patiently and wait for her to finish thinking.

Finally, she murmurs, "I guess it can't hurt."

"It's not supposed to, and if the guy you're having sex with knows what he's doing, it'll actually feel pretty damn epic." Unless the participants want it to hurt, but that's way outside the scope of this conversation. "Trust me, I'll do everything I can to make this good for you . . .

if you'll let me."

She nods slowly. "I will."

"I'm attracted to you, Jenna. I find you sexy and smart, and I want to fuck you. Do you want that too?"

She licks her lips. "Yes."

With a victorious grin, I stalk back across the room to the bed. "Then come here," I growl. I haul her up onto her knees into the most searing kiss I can manage. No more going slow and chaste—I'm going to take her like I've wanted to all night.

A half gasp, half moan escapes her and I smirk against her lips. *Nice to know I haven't lost my touch. And speaking of touch . . .*

As my tongue explores her mouth, I reach around her supple back to unclasp her bra. I pull it down over her arms and let myself drink in the feel of her bare torso pressed against my chest. Full breasts, plush and heavy, silky-soft skin, topped with already-hardening nipples . . . damn, I just have to get a taste.

Jenna stifles a disappointed noise when I abandon

her mouth, only to sigh in bliss as I kiss down her jaw, her neck, over her collarbone, and then to my prize. I suck and lick at one of those pretty pink nipples, rolling the other between my thumb and finger.

Her moans soon escalate to needy cries. I work my free hand lower and run my fingers along her cleft, feeling the wetness I'd sought earlier. Her hips stutter forward and my cock gives an answering twitch. *Oh, hell yeah, now we're talking.* I delve in, slicking two fingers, and slide them back and forth over her clit. She whimpers and clutches at my shoulders, trembling with each pass.

Her shivers abruptly ramp up, her whole body quaking. *Shit, already?* My cock throbs. I only intended to tease her, but it looks like I did a little too good of a job. I rub her through her orgasm until she flinches and sags against my shoulders. I ease her back onto the bed where she sits down with her knees splayed, still breathing fast, her eyes wide.

"Poor thing, you must've been pent up," I purr. "How long has it been since someone gave you what you deserve?"

All she says is, "Fuck." She sounds dazed.

I hold back a laugh. "That's the plan. Now ... are you ready for more?"

"Absolutely," she says, her voice still weak, but husky. Already eager for more.

I grin and dive in for another deep kiss. *Tonight is going to be fun.*

Chapter Nine

Jenna

Sweating, I gulp down air thick with the smell of sex. I tremble on my hands and knees, arching my back to offer my ass, my face pressed against the mattress. Emmett's hot, muscular weight covers me. One hand grips my hip tight, pulling me back to meet him with every forceful thrust, and the other works between my thighs, rubbing my clit.

His pleasure is merciless. The angle lets him pound deep inside me and he knows exactly where to aim, his cock striking directly into my G-spot hard and fast, delivering jolt after jolt of white heat through my entire body. It's almost too intense. I've already come twice tonight, but I can feel yet another orgasm building, the tension gradually winding tighter, stealing my breath and filling my veins with fire.

"Just one more time, Jenna." His voice, gone dark and rough with passion, drips sin into my ear. "You can do it. Come for me. Let me feel you."

My body has seized control and it's unashamedly greedy for more, taking everything I've been denied for years. I struggle to speak.

"Don't . . . stop . . ."

"Never, sweetheart," he pants out.

My toes curl and my hands scrabble at the sheets. I don't care about the inappropriate endearment. I barely process what he's saying at all. The approach of ecstasy dominates my awareness completely.

"Fuck." Emmett curses behind me, his voice deep and rough. "Gonna come now."

The muscles in his thighs stiffen and his cock jerks with his release—powerful, hot stream after stream of semen.

I cry out as my third orgasm of the night crashes over me like a tsunami. All my muscles lock so hard, I quake. The incredible sensation keeps coming in wave after overwhelming wave. He keeps fucking me through it, letting me squeeze out every drop of this bliss, until I whimper with overstimulation. Only then does he gently withdraw his cock and remove his fingers. I melt into a puddle on the mattress, still gasping for breath.

Sex has never been like this. Even in my wildest fantasies.

Lying down on his side, Emmett props himself up on his elbow to look at me. With a smirk, he asks, "So, would you say I delivered?"

I nod slowly, still dazed. Holy shit, did he ever.

That might literally have been the best sex of my life. I'm so glad I decided to give him a chance to work his magic. Hell, a tiny part of me is hoping his sperm doesn't take right away, just so we can keep trying.

He pulls me onto him as he gently rolls onto his back, my cheek resting on his pectoral. My instinct is to pull back ... but he's so warm, and surprisingly comfortable. I almost want to close my eyes and just listen to his heartbeat, breathe in his masculine smell of sweat and sex and crisp cologne. Maybe even fall asleep on him.

But we can't cuddle, and we definitely can't spend the whole night together. It would confuse our relationship way too much, no matter how tempting the afterglow makes the idea. So, I force myself to roll off him.

"Hmm?" The mattress dips behind me as he sits up.

I grab my fleece bathrobe from the hook on the back of the door. "You were right. That was pretty fun," I say as breezily as I can, keeping my back turned to him until I'm safely covered. "Thanks for the fertilization."

He grumbles again, this time sounding dissatisfied. I cinch my robe's belt tight and wince at the tiny sting of soreness at my injection site.

"What is it?" Emmett asks, swinging his legs over the side of the mattress.

I shrug and gather my blouse, jeans, and underthings from where I dropped them on the floor in the dark. "It's nothing. Just a little sore from the shot I gave myself."

"Damn. I didn't know you had to do that." The tenderness in his voice is so uncharacteristically sweet that it makes my heart squeeze. "Can I see?"

Stepping closer to where he's seated on the bed, I untie the robe and stand before him.

Emmett places his large hands on my hips and leans in to press a soft kiss right over the little red mark.

"All better," I murmur, my voice soft.

After that, Emmett gets up and retrieves his clothes too, though with clear reluctance.

It's obvious he's accepted that he has to leave. I'm relieved—I was a little worried he might make this difficult—while also strangely disappointed that he's so blasé about me pushing him out of here.

But I can't have any of that nonsense. *It's good he knows the game plan*, I tell myself. It doesn't take a psychologist to figure out that my fear of starting a real relationship is deeply rooted in the trauma of my father leaving when I was a child. It's also not something I want to deal with now. I have my life, and my goals, and I'm perfectly content with that.

After a minute of silent dressing, he asks, "When will you know?"

Now that I'm halfway decent again, I turn to face him. "I'll take a pregnancy test in two weeks. But, uh ... it'll increase the odds if we do it again. Are you free tomorrow, by any chance?"

That puts a smile back on his handsome face right away. "I'll make time. Okay if we meet at my place? I can get there from the office faster."

I hesitate, then nod slowly. "I don't see why not."

Once he's hidden away his distracting nudity, I escort him back to the front door and hand him his coat. "See you after work," I say, then an uneasy thought occurs to me. "Will you be okay getting home? Should I call you a cab?" I don't want him to sleep over, but it *is* awfully late, after all, and I'd feel horrible if something happened.

"Isn't it typically the man who offers that?" Smirking, he sees my look of surprise. "Don't worry, I'll be fine." He pauses, his hand on the knob. His smile is off somehow. Not like the strained smile of an awkward situation, but . . . reluctant?

Whatever it is, something about it makes me lean forward. I peck him gently, chastely, on the cheek. "Okay, then. Good night."

The crinkles at the corners of his eyes deepen. "Good night to you too."

He shuts the door behind him. I lock it . . . then, for a moment, I linger there in my bathrobe before going to brush my teeth.

I still don't know why I gave him that one last kiss, but it felt right. Like it was the least I could do.

I mean, what was I supposed to do, shake his hand? Thank him for his above-and-beyond performance and promise to leave him a good review on Yelp? Come on. After he's put up with all my weird requirements so gracefully—not to mention blowing my mind for hours—a kiss is only appropriate.

Never mind. I'm overthinking things again. Time to get back in bed, and this time, use it for its intended purpose.

• • •

My sleep is deep and dreamless. The next morning, I drift awake half an hour before my alarm. I shut it off, then sit up and stretch luxuriously, smiling almost without realizing it. I can't remember the last time I slept so soundly or woke up feeling so peppy.

I swing my legs out of bed and hop right into the shower. My hip and thigh muscles twinge and my core is still sore, but I don't mind too much—those little aches and pains are souvenirs of the incredible workout Emmett gave me. I hum a cheerful tune as I shampoo and blow-dry my hair.

While getting dressed, I glance at the clock and am pleasantly surprised. Waking up early and bouncing around with such energy has put me ahead of schedule. Normally, I just have a bowl of cereal or grab something from the coffee shop on the corner, but today I think I have time to cook breakfast. My stomach growls its enthusiasm at the idea. Guess I worked up an appetite last night.

I brew a cup of coffee, scramble a couple of eggs, and eat them on toast. After the dirty dishes are in the dishwasher, I start to put on makeup, then pause. For some reason, I feel like primping a little more today. I swap my usual nude palette for dark green eyeshadow, shades of pink on my cheeks, and a swipe of my favorite lipstick over my mouth.

The results make me smile. Maybe I should do this more often.

Unbidden, the thought of whether Emmett would

like it jumps into my mind. I shake my head—*who cares what he thinks of my face?*—and leave for work.

The store is still dark when I pull into the parking lot. I unlock the doors, flick on the lights, turn the sign around, and open the shop. I check the cash register, even though I know there's enough change in the drawer since we only had one customer yesterday, and I counted the money at closing. It's been a while since we accumulated enough cash to squirrel away in the office safe.

The door jingles, and without bothering to look up from my meager handful of bills, I call out, "Good morning, Britt."

"Hello, Jenna," she calls back.

Yep, I knew it was her. The odds of a customer coming in are practically zero at any time, let alone first thing in the morning. But that fact doesn't depress me quite as much as usual. My spot of morning sunshine hasn't worn off yet, I guess.

Britt joins me behind the counter. "You seem like you're in a good mood today," she comments way too innocently. "Anything nice happen?"

I raise an eyebrow at her slightly. "What's that supposed to mean?"

"Nothing," she says in a tone that suggests she means *everything*.

I replace the money in the register drawer and shove it back in with a *ching*. "Is it really so unusual for me to be in a good mood?"

She opens her mouth, closes it, then opens it again. "Well . . . uh, no offense, but it actually kind of is." When I blink at her, she rushes to explain. "Don't get me wrong, I'm not complaining, I just—"

I chuckle. "It's okay, I'm not offended. I was just surprised."

She huffs a sheepish little titter. "What I meant was, it seems like you're always so stressed out, worrying about the shop and everything. So it's nice to see you happy for once."

"That's sweet. Thanks." I beam at her. "If you must know, last night . . ." I drop my gaze for a moment, still smiling in a slightly silly way. "I went on a date. Sort of."

By which, I mean a living sex god flew down from heaven and fucked me seven ways to Sunday.

Britt's face breaks out in a huge grin. "I knew it! Whoo, get it, girl!" Then her brow furrows. "Wait, what do you mean, sort of?"

I shrug helplessly. "It's complicated." The understatement of the century.

"Why? Is he married or something?"

"Oh, come on," I say with a snort.

"I know you wouldn't do that. I'm just curious."

I fiddle with my pen. "I guess it's the opposite, actually—it *can't* get complicated."

Britt squints at me. "Huh?"

"I don't have room in my life for a relationship right now. My goals are to get pregnant and dig this shop out of the grave, nothing else."

Comprehension dawns over her face. "Oh. Ohhh. *Oh.*"

Oops . . . I said the P-word. That may have been

slightly more information than I wanted to let slip. Oh well, too late now. Britt already knew I've been wanting to have a baby anyway. So, I just shrug and leave it at, "Yeah."

"So, you're . . . okay, I get it now. It's a no-strings-attached kinda thing." She looks aside for a moment. "Sorry. I didn't mean to pry."

I wave my hand. "No, it's fine. Pry away."

Five months ago, Britt told me she'd finally managed to kick out her evil roommate, and my response was to take her out for tequila shots. Outside of signing her paychecks, our relationship is more like friends than the standard boss-employee dynamic.

"Really? In that case . . ." The grin flashes back. "Do you like him? Is he cute? Is he nice?"

I should be a little embarrassed to be squealing over boys like we're at a high-school slumber party. Instead, I laugh. "Yes to all, so far."

She follows me to my office in the rear of the store. "Then why not hang on to him?"

"Britt . . ." I sigh as I sit down at my desk.

She holds up her hands, still not understanding but accepting. "Well, whatever's going on, I'm glad you met someone. And I hope he keeps acting like a good guy, because I like seeing you this way."

"Thanks, but he's only sticking around until I'm pregnant. It's nothing more than a barter arrangement, a trading-goods-for-services kind of thing."

Britt chuckles. "If you say so."

I boot up our store computer, open its email—and my positive attitude goes down in flames. Squatting right at the top of my in-box like an ugly toad is another offer letter from Baxter Books.

"Jesus," I mutter.

Britt leans forward to read over my shoulder and growls in dismay at the number visible in the email's preview line. "These assholes can't even come up with a decent price," she huffs. "They're offering pennies on the dollar! How rude . . . they have some serious balls even proposing a figure that low. If they think we're so worthless, why have they been crawling up our ass constantly for months?"

I delete the email, and if I'd clicked any harder, I would have broken the poor mouse. "Even if they were offering ten times my startup costs, I still wouldn't sell. Those Baxter pricks don't have a clue what we're doing here. They don't understand the value of antique books. We're trying to preserve and celebrate real art, the living history of literature, but all they care about is profits." I shake my head in frustration. "Ugh, they're just heartless. Corporate robots. They would gut this place. Turn it into yet another cookie-cutter, mega-chain, big-box *mausoleum*—" I punctuate every word by jabbing my finger at the computer screen. "And ruin everything it stands for."

Britt is nodding along emphatically. "Damn right. Maybe you should write that speech down and send it to them."

"No, I don't want to dignify this crap with a response." I push out my chair and stand up. "Even if it would be really satisfying. Come on, let's finish opening this place."

Before I can follow Britt out to the sales floor, my phone pings and I grab it from my purse to find a text from Emmett.

Can't wait to have you in my bed tonight.

Suddenly, my mood is a little brighter.

• • •

As the day goes on, my good mood revives. Partly because we get an unprecedented three whole customers . . . but mostly, I realize, because of the prospect of seeing Emmett again tonight. By four thirty, I catch myself drumming my fingers on my desk. At five sharp, I reapply my lipstick and flip the sign around and lock the door, and then I'm off like a bat out of hell.

My heart beats faster as I drive to the address he gave me earlier. Why am I so hyped up? Am I nervous? I can't be nervous. He's already seen every inch of my naked, writhing body—now is an odd time to suddenly get shy. Or am I just that excited to fuck him again? I never thought of myself as such a horndog, but even after three earth-shattering orgasms not even twenty-four hours ago, I'm still eager for more.

I find a spot in the parking garage under the building and ride the elevator to the penthouse suite. Emmett opens the door at my first knock. He flashes me one of his trademark grins and my stomach gives a little flip.

"Hi, I'm here," I say, unable to think of anything wittier.

"I'm glad." His gaze lingers on my mouth, and I see the hint of a smile on his lips. "Come on in."

Emmett leads me through the entry hall to the main living area. I try not to gawk too much, but damn, this place is unbelievable. Intricately patterned parquet floors, bay windows with a breathtaking view of the city skyline, furnished in a classy modern style. The rooms are so cavernous, the ceilings so high, the click of my heels on the hardwood actually echoes.

I suddenly feel a tiny bit intimidated.

He pauses in front of an elegant black-and-white leather couch that looks like it cost more than my first car. "You want to go get some dinner first?" He glances across the living room into the kitchen. "I don't think I have anything here to eat, but there's some amazing restaurants nearby. Just about every kind of cuisine under the sun."

I shake my head. Even if my stomach wasn't jumping around like crazy, I don't want to get too familiar with him. We've already had two dates, and that's two more than necessary. "No thanks, I'm not hungry right now. I can grab a bite on my way home."

A line appears between his eyebrows. He looks like he wants to argue, but instead he just says, "If you insist. Then, please, make yourself at home."

Everything looks so expensive, I'm almost scared to touch it. But I obey and sit on the couch, running my fingers over the buttery-soft leather in appreciation.

He sits down beside me, barely a breath away, and rests his hand on mine. "Can I get you anything to drink?"

I can feel his body heat. My mouth has gone dry, and a drink isn't what I want. "No thanks," I repeat. I want him.

There's a slight frown on his face. But his displeasure evaporates when I close the distance between us, pressing my lips to his. I let the kiss linger, openmouthed, tantalizing. An invitation, a promise.

"I see," he murmurs. "You want to get straight to the main event."

"Is that okay?" I reply, my lips brushing against his.

"I can get on board with that." He kisses me back, hard and hungry. Then he takes my hand and leads me down the hall to the master bedroom.

Chapter Ten

Emmett

As soon as we're inside my bedroom, I devour Jenna's mouth. She moans and starts tearing at my clothes.

I can't get her naked fast enough. I kiss and suck and nip at her breasts, laving her pebbled nipples with my tongue. She arches into me like she's been waiting for this all day, just like I have, then pulls me backward onto the bed, on top of her. Kissing her deeply, I caress the soft skin of her inner thighs, teasing as I get closer to the lovely place between them, doing my best to melt her into a pliant mess.

When her sighs turn shaky, I spread her legs, putting her on full display. Wet and ready ... gorgeous. I take a moment to admire the view before pushing her knees up to her chest.

I press my hips forward and let out a broken moan as I press the head of my cock into her tight, slick heat. Fuck, I hope I never get used to the sensation of bareback fucking ... Jenna has spoiled me for condoms. She answers with a throaty, lilting noise, her toes curling. I sink in deeper, loving every new sensation.

At last, the back of her thighs touch my stomach and I'm buried to the hilt. With every thrust, she arches up to meet me, her red-painted lips parting in bliss, and I've never seen anything so hot in my life. Her sultry moans hit me like whiskey. I love the heady, desperate noises she makes when I stroke her clit. I drink in every delicious shudder of her prone body.

"That's it," I say, peppering her neck with kisses and bites. "Let me hear your voice. Tell me how good you're feeling."

She wails out a shapeless sound that could be "more."

I obey and push my hips harder, giving her everything I have. She moans, louder this time, and rakes her nails down my back. The slight pain only enhances my pleasure by contrast. Jenna under me, around me, is the best part of this week. Just to see her so passionately unhinged, our breaths panting and mingling. My blood is so hot for her, this woman who crawled into bed yesterday so quiet and resigned, but now is completely reckless with want.

"You're so sexy like this," I growl into her ear. "So . . . good." I can't resist the urge to suck a bruise into that soft, tender skin on her neck.

God, she feels so incredible it almost hurts, her pussy muscles fluttering around my cock, drawing me deeper in, and then, *oh fuck*, she's clamping down hard in rhythmic waves and I'm past the point of no return. A ragged groan rises from deep in my chest. I bury myself even deeper inside as I plunge headlong after her into orgasm.

Still panting, I pull out and see the evidence of our lovemaking on her pink flesh. It's the hottest thing I've ever seen. My chest fills with animalistic pride. *My seed in my woman.* I like that thought way too much, and I'm too lost in lust to push it away.

The sight of her, the sounds she makes, the way she feels, it's like a fever that engulfs me. Visceral, irresistible. I need to make her come again . . . come so hard, so many times, no one else will ever be good enough for her.

She drags me up and kisses me hungrily. A primal light flashes in her half-lidded eyes. I can tell she doesn't need a moment of rest, and fortunately, neither do I. Our bodies demand more of each other ... more pleasure, more sweat, and more of my seed. And I give it to her.

Jenna's orgasms always seem to overwhelm her. Her eyes flutter shut, then fly open, and she gasps *wow* or *oh my God*, like she's shocked by how good it feels. Like she didn't know sex could be so enjoyable.

What kind of crappy lovers has she put up with? I'm almost angry at every man who's ever touched her—not because they came before me, but because they clearly didn't give her what she deserved. It's a crime that such an amazing woman has been deprived of good sex for so long. So, every time she comes, I take it as a personal challenge to push her to even more orgasms, even greater heights of pleasure.

When our passion finally simmers down from a boil to quiet completion, I take the chance to gather her into my arms. Now she looks warm and hazy, softened in the afterglow. She strikes me as a woman who doesn't often let herself slow down, let alone stop and be lazy and content—something else we have in common. She offers me a sated little half smile, and I return it.

Then she rolls over to the edge of the bed. "Sorry to run so soon, but . . ."

I can't help the frown that pulls on my lips. I don't want her to just rush off again. "Hey, where's the fire?" I ask, sitting up.

"I have to drive home, figure out some dinner, and get to sleep so I can function at work tomorrow." She leans down to pick up her bra and starts pulling it on.

I rest my hand on her still-bare shoulder. "Sleep is overrated, and I have food here. Or we could walk down to my favorite café and order breakfast for dinner."

A stone forms in my stomach during the moments of silence that follow my suggestion.

She considers it, her mouth pressing into a line. "Pancakes actually sound pretty tempting. There's probably nothing good in my fridge anyway."

"Pancakes it is, then."

I'm pleased to score what is technically a third date. I enjoy talking with Jenna as much as I enjoy trying to knock her up. And I like how *normal* it feels to eat together and do other things besides fuck. It may sound strange, but I haven't met a woman whose company I truly enjoy outside the bedroom in a long time. I may as well savor it while it lasts.

After we're dressed, we walk down the street a few blocks to the café. After we've ordered, I lean toward her over the small table. "So, how was work today?" Then I shake my head. "Wait, never mind, you said you don't like talking about work. What *would* you like to talk about?"

She considers for a moment. "Tell me . . . what do you like to do for fun?"

"What we're doing now is pretty fun. It's sort of my number-one thing to do for fun, truth be told." My smile crooks into a smirk.

She gives me a gently exasperated look. "I meant other than seeing women."

"Usually work takes all my time, but every once in a blue moon, I manage to get away from the city and go camping or hiking."

She blinks. "You're a nature lover?"

"Oh yeah, big time." I raise an eyebrow teasingly. "Why do you sound surprised?"

"I admit, it's a little tough to picture you in hiking boots and canvas shorts. I've never seen you in anything less than business casual."

"You've seen me in a lot less, actually."

She chuckles. "You know I meant other than naked. So, how did you get into that? Not exactly the easiest hobby for a city boy."

"I don't often get time to go anymore, but yeah, the outdoors is a major stress reliever for me."

I must not have been able to keep the disappointment from my voice. Something about Jenna makes it easy to overshare ... but I shouldn't give in to the impulse. This is supposed to be a lighthearted fling, and talking about childhood disappointments is the very opposite of fun.

I lean back and force a casual tone. "Even though I had to study business in college so I could take over when Dad retired, I took so many classes in stuff like canyoneering and ecology, I ended up declaring a second major in outdoor tourism. So, if you ever want to know the best way to fall off a mountain or what plants you can eat if you're lost in the woods, then I'm your guy." I chuckle, but it comes out half-assed, and I figure it's time to change the subject. "Since we're talking ancient history . . . how did you get to be such a bookworm?"

"Childhood is ancient history? Hey, what're you implying about my age?" She smiles to let me know she's just kidding and isn't really insulted. "I don't know. I've just always loved reading. My dad . . ." She stops with her mouth still open, closes it, then resumes. "My mom was always working and I was an only child, so books kept me company. Typical latchkey kid."

I stop myself from digging deeper into that Freudian slip since she clearly doesn't want to share. I, of all people, can understand one's father being a sore subject. Besides, I'm not supposed to care in the first place. I'm not supposed to want to get closer—I mean, I don't want to. It's just simple curiosity. That's absolutely all it is.

But there is something else I can't stop myself from asking. "Speaking of your mom . . . she called you when we first met?"

"Oh God, don't remind me." Jenna laughs instead of groaning, though it's clearly not such a horrible memory anymore.

"Sorry," I say with a chuckle. I'm not really sorry, not about the events that led me to sitting here in this restaurant with Jenna after a night of wild sex. "But she knows about your . . . plans?"

She nods matter-of-factly, as if there's nothing unusual about it. "Yep. Her attitude is, she raised me alone and I turned out fine, so she figures I can pull off single motherhood too."

Interesting . . . implying the Dad Who Must Not Be Named either died or ran off. Either way, I can see why she doesn't want to talk about him. "She sounds like a cool lady," I say.

Jenna chuckles. "I don't know if 'cool' is the word I'd use. She likes crocheting, kitten figurines, and reality shows. But hard as nails? Take no shit? That's my mom."

I laugh and almost say, *I'd like to meet her someday.* But at the last second, I swallow it. Getting to know Jenna's family isn't in the cards for us. How would she even introduce us? *Hi, Mom, this is the guy who agreed to impregnate me.*

Instead, I say, "I'm sure she's right. You can handle anything."

Jenna's smile is appreciative and vulnerable and far too beautiful. "Thanks. I hope so."

The pancakes arrive and we dig in with gusto, still chatting away. Our conversation winds on late into the night, and eventually Jenna glances at the time on her phone.

"I should probably say good night," she says at last with a wry twist of her mouth. "I have to get up early for work tomorrow."

"I'll walk you back to your car." I stand and offer my arm, and she takes it without hesitation.

We stroll through the quiet city streets together to my building. I follow her to her car, say good night one last time, and watch her drive away. Then I take the elevator upstairs to my empty penthouse.

As I walk down the hall, I remember how Jenna's

presence earlier seemed to fill the silence. She warmed this place.

I strip naked and get into bed. It's gone cold by now, but the sheets still smell like her. Her sweat, her pleasure, her light floral perfume.

I stare at the pattern of shadows on the ceiling. Unbidden, the thought comes that this place is too big for just one person. It's not the first time I've had that thought, but for some reason, tonight I can't push it away like I usually do. Four thousand square feet is a little excessive for one person, I knew that when I bought the place, but it seemed fitting for the lifestyle I live. Always doing what's expected of me, yet never doing what I want. A sense of melancholy takes over as I reflect on my future—or lack of a future—with Jenna.

We entered this strange little un-relationship to get Jenna pregnant. But once I succeed . . . I'm going to miss this warmth, I realize. Jesse was right. I don't normally date women who are my age, or so smart and career-driven, or so sassy and kind in equal measure. Jenna stimulates me in many more ways than just physical.

No, dumbass, this isn't dating, I think, correcting myself.

We aren't in this for the romance. Really, we can't even become friends. We agreed right off the bat that we'd stay out of each other's lives. The instant she pees on a stick and sees the plus sign she's been longing for, it's all over.

My life is about fulfilling obligations, doing what's expected of me, and this is what Jenna wants and expects from me. Nothing more. That thought alone is enough to give me pause.

Rolling over, I shut my eyes. *Enjoy this while it lasts, Emmett, and then move on.*

Just like you do with everything else.

Chapter Eleven

Jenna

My pregnancy test appointment crawls closer. I itch with curiosity and anticipation, but I force myself to be patient and wait out the two weeks instead of raiding the corner drugstore for pee sticks.

I didn't plan on contacting Emmett until I knew whether I needed another dose of sperm, but some combination of restlessness and horniness compels me to text him a few days after our last "meeting." Before I know it, we're texting every few days, although usually just to complain about work.

At home one night, I'm alternating browsing baby supplies online, trying not to eat a second bowl of butter pecan ice cream, and talking to Emmett. I've been in a shitty mood all week, and work today only made it worse. Luckily, Emmett understands. His company is apparently going through a rough merger with the competition, which only cements my conviction that selling out is the wrong thing to do.

After an hour of mutual bitching, I'm starting to feel somewhat better—until I go to the bathroom and find a big, fat, ugly red streak in the crotch of my panties. There's even a slight smear on my white leggings, just to add insult to injury.

Dammit, this is the freaking icing on the cake.

I stare at the mocking stain. Everything makes sense now. Mood swings, food cravings, feeling fat and tired, wanting to drag Emmett back into my bed . . . I let hope lead me astray. I've been deluding myself into interpreting everything as pregnancy symptoms when it was just goddamn PMS.

I have never inserted a tampon so angrily in my life.

I ball up my bloodstained clothes and slam-dunk them into the hamper. Fuck my entire life. I need alcohol. I'm one hundred percent baby-free, so I'm allowed to drink. Hell, I'm entitled.

I change into a fresh outfit—with black leggings this time because, fuck you, Aunt Flo—pack up my purse, and head for the nearest bar, Crossroads Tavern. I've only been there a few times, but it's a decent enough watering hole, and more importantly, it's nearby so I can walk there. Drinking enough to dull my emotions without having to worry about driving home is my top priority right now.

The bar is packed, and as I squeeze inside, I see why. Everyone's attention is glued to the big-screen televisions blaring a championship basketball game. Oh, whatever. I'm just here to drown my sorrows—as long as I can find somewhere to sit, I don't care how noisy it is.

I shoulder my way through to the bar and shout over the noise of the crowd, "Double shot of tequila, please. And I want to open a tab."

The bartender nods and trades me my order for my credit card. I take a gulp, shuddering at the burn, then sigh at the sweet warmth that spreads through my veins.

The crowd erupts in earsplitting clapping and hollering. Someone must have scored a crucial basket. Even though I don't follow either of the teams playing, I turn my attention to the nearest television, just for something for my eyeballs to do while I drink. But I've barely finished my order before that gets too boring.

On a tequila-lubricated impulse, I pull out my phone and text Emmett: *Hey, party at Crossroads, you in?* I throw in a couple of random emojis for good measure, then get back to drinking.

I've polished off another tequila shot when a hand lands on my lower back. I whip around, prepared to deck whatever random asshole is trying to grope me, and stop short at the sight of Emmett. Looking agitated, he yells something unintelligible over the ruckus.

"What?" I shout.

"You shouldn't be drinking," he shouts back.

"I can do what I want." My third shot arrives—or does it count as my fourth, since the first was a double? Doesn't matter. I toss it down my throat.

"But what about the baby?" he insists.

My stomach squirms. "I can't hear you," I lie.

Emmett casts a frustrated glare at the huge, rowdy crowd. "Oh, this is ridiculous. Let's get out of here."

I set my jaw. "No. I want to get drunk."

"You're already drunk. I'm walking you home."

Who does he think he is, my boss? I glare at him. "Fuck off."

"Maybe later. Come on." He calls to the bartender, "Excuse me, can I get her tab? I'm paying."

I growl, but the bartender hands over my card, so I pocket it and grudgingly let Emmett drag me out of the bar. The sidewalk tilts under my feet but he holds me tight, not letting me fall to the pavement in a heap.

"What the hell is up with you tonight?" Emmett asks, staring urgently at me.

He has such pretty eyes. Like rich dark chocolate . . . and I'd kill for those long lashes.

"Hey, are you listening?"

Not really. "It's fine," I snap.

"But what if—"

"I'm not fucking pregnant, okay? I got my period. Happy?"

All the confused irritation instantly falls from his face. "Oh," he says, his voice flat.

"Yeah." Even though the quick motion makes me sway slightly, I look away, not wanting him to see how deeply this failure stings.

Before I know what's going on, he pulls me into a tight hug. "I'm sorry."

I stiffen, not expecting his comfort, then melt into it. The warm, solid strength of his arms brings a knot to my throat. My anger abruptly dissolves into being just plain upset. "It's not fair," I mumble, sniffing into his shoulder.

"I know," he says gently.

"I t-tried so hard, I did all this shit, and it still didn't work." I know I'm whining, acting ridiculous, but right now I don't care. If only for a few minutes, I feel like being fussed over. I feel like being a girly-girl who cries and gets emotional. "What'm I gonna do?"

He pets my back in long, calming strokes, as if I were a cat. "We can try again. For as long as it takes."

"You're being so nice to me."

"Of course. We're friends." His hand pauses on my back for a second. "I mean, seeing you like this, who wouldn't want to cheer you up?"

If I were any less sad and drunk and just generally discombobulated, I would start overanalyzing everything about this situation. But all I want right now is his comfort and concern.

No . . . that's still not completely true. I don't want just anyone's sympathy. I want Emmett, and I don't give a shit how it happens.

He leans away without breaking the hug, just enough to look in my eyes. "Feel better?"

I manage another long, wet sniff, and nod. "Yeah. Thanks."

And I actually do . . . better enough, in fact, for my mind to return to the problem at hand. There must be something more we can do, some way we can make sure we take a better stab at pregnancy next time. The alcohol-soaked gears start turning.

Smiling, he brushes a stray hair out of my eyes. "I'm glad I could help y—"

"How often do you jerk off?" I say, interrupting him.

He blinks several times. "What?"

I step back slightly to pull a tissue from my purse and blow my nose. "Jacking off can lower your sperm count, y'know. So, how often?"

"I-I'm not telling you that," he sputters.

I cock my eyebrow. "So it's a lot."

"No. When someone says, 'No comment,' it doesn't automatically mean the most incriminating possible answer."

"Fine. Doesn't matter anyway. Going forward, next month, I want to institute a new policy ... all of your orgasms belong to me." I pull his hand down to cup my crotch. "Anytime you need to relieve pressure, you're only allowed to use my pussy."

His eyes get wider with every word, and his mouth opens and closes a few times. When he removes his hand, he seems reluctant.

"You listening?" I demand.

"Yeah, I heard every word. Believing them was the

hard part."

I cross my arms over my chest. "Well, believe it. Yes or no?"

He licks his lips in what could be trepidation, but I hope is eagerness. Damn, he has some nice lips. Full, soft. I'd like those lips to go places.

What was I talking about again?

Finally, he replies, "If that's what has to happen, then . . . I guess I can do that."

I pump my fist in drunken victory and wince when my lower belly protests with a cramp. Agreeing on a plan has cheered me right up. More sex has got to equal more chance at a baby, right? And the prospect of hopping back into bed with Emmett is like winning the lottery.

"Is something still bothering you?" he asks, his voice warm with concern.

"Nothing's wrong. It's just some cramps. No big deal."

Some distant part of me is sober enough to wonder why I blurted it out like that. Normally, I'd hesitate to talk about Private Uterus Things with a man who's not my boyfriend—hell, even some of my old boyfriends were jerks about it. But Emmett doesn't seem grossed out, only sympathetic. And somehow, I knew he wouldn't mind. Things have always been different with Emmett. Comfortable. Like I can share anything at all and he not only won't react badly, he'll actually give a shit about how I feel.

Must be because of our totally all-about-medical-stuff arrangement, and not at all about the way he smiles. We're just friends. Not even friend-friends. Sex friends. Very sexy friends.

Shut up, *brain.*

Before I realize it, we're walking, and soon we're almost back to my apartment.

Emmett interrupts my increasingly dirty thoughts by suggesting, "Maybe I can lend a hand."

I unlock the door and he follows me inside. We're standing in my foyer, with only the dim lamp I left on to light our surroundings.

When I look up at Emmett, I see he has that gleam in his eye that I've learned to recognize. The sly, sensual look that means he's cooking up some naughty scheme. But what he's up to specifically, I have no idea.

"What could you do about cramps?" I ask. "You have some ibuprofen on you?"

"Nope." He cups me hard through my leggings.

I gasp. "W-what are you doing?" Looks like he meant *lend a hand* very literally. My body votes yes . . . but the few brain cells that survived the tequila can't forget the fact that I'm on my period and should be closed for business.

His fingers slide over my covered crotch, caressing up and down, making it hard for me to think. "Orgasms release endorphins and soothe menstrual cramps. It's scientifically proven."

"Oh, so y-you're a gynecologist now?" My attempt at snark is undermined by the way his skilled teasing makes my voice shake. Damn, he hasn't even touched my clit directly yet, but it's already starting to ache.

"I dabble." He licks the shell of my ear, making me shudder.

"But . . ." I sigh.

He presses me back against the wall, sandwiching me between its cool surface and his heat. "Let me make you feel better."

I give in and roll my hips into his touch.

With a pleased sound in my ear, he slides his hand down into my panties. His fingers feel cool on my overheated flesh. I scoot my feet apart to give him more room to work—and oh, work he does. His fingers rub circles into my swollen bud as he kisses and nips a sensitive spot on my neck, sending tingles down my spine. I don't care that we shouldn't anymore. I'm drunk and horny, I want pleasure, I want Emmett.

"You like it?" His voice has turned low and rough.

"Mmm," I murmur, panting. "Yes."

I can't hold back my whimpers. I bury my face in his broad shoulder and spread my legs wider for his exploring hand. My knees threaten to buckle, but I know he won't let me fall. Ecstasy rolls through me and I bite down on the crook of his neck, muffling my cries. Emmett sucks in his breath and his steely erection nudges my stomach.

I come in a dizzying rush of endorphins that really do make me feel better—from head to toe.

When my trembling subsides, he presses a soft, almost tender kiss to my lips. "I'll knock you up next month, I promise," he says softly. "But for now . . . it's time to get you to bed."

His warm arm around my lower back steadies me as I toe off my shoes, and I realize I'm not depressed about getting my period anymore. In fact, I'm excited about what the next month holds—an open buffet of Emmett.

Chapter Twelve

Emmett

Late at night, I toss and turn, restless and horny. What I usually do in these situations is jack off, but breaking my promise to Jenna isn't an option. I have to keep my hands off my dick, no matter how hard things get . . . pun very much intended.

I roll over to grab my phone from the nightstand, check my calendar, and suppress a groan of impatient despair. It's only been a week since her period . . . it'll be at least that long before she's due for her next impregnation attempt. And I didn't get off the last time I saw her either. Which makes it about two weeks since I've had any release. I didn't quite realize how stressed out I would be ignoring my cock.

No way in hell can I wait out that whole time. I need to see Jenna ahead of schedule. But calling her at this hour is out of the question—I'd just wake her up and piss her off. I also shouldn't bug her while she's at work tomorrow. I decide to wait until the next evening. Surely, I can make it through just one more measly day at the office, right?

Yeah, about that.

All through the next morning, I struggle to keep my mind on my work. It just keeps sliding off the dry memos and reports and graphs into longing, pornographic thoughts of Jenna. What's she doing right now? Does she still want me? How long will it be until she calls for me again?

My control frays thin . . . then, around lunchtime, finally snaps. *Fuck it.* I give up. I can't take this anymore. I buzz Lisa to tell her to hold all calls and visitors for fifteen minutes, then pull out my phone to call Jenna. I drum my fingers on my desk while it rings and rings.

Finally, she picks up. "Emmett?" she asks, sounding distracted. "What's going on?"

I guess this is the first time I've called her instead of texted, let alone in the middle of the workday, but I did it because I need a response as soon as possible. "Yeah, it's me. Listen . . . what are you doing tonight?"

"Why?" Skepticism colors her voice.

Casually, I reply, "Just wondering if you're up for another date night."

A long pause, during which the already minimal background noise fades completely. She must have retreated to privacy. "This is a booty call?" she asks, now with a trace of what I hope is curiosity, but I think is actually annoyance.

Yep, this conversation clearly isn't going at all the way I wanted it to. I rub the back of my neck. "Well, I wouldn't have picked those exact words, but sure."

"It's the middle of the day. I'm at work . . . actually, aren't you too? Why did you booty-call me now?"

I shrug, even though she can't see me. "Why do you think? Booty calls have a pretty specific purpose."

"Okay, everybody stop saying booty call. I'm asking because my next ovulation isn't for a while yet, and assuming you have a calendar, you already knew that. So, not that I'm offended by the offer or anything, but I just can't figure out why you want to fuck me."

I almost laugh. Why would I ever *not* want to fuck her? Wait . . . I have an inkling of what's going on here. "Did you forget what we talked about the last time I saw you?" She was practically falling over, so she might have been too drunk to remember the details of our conversation.

"Uh ... maybe?" A rustle in the background, like she's looking through papers. "Sorry. Can you be more specific?"

I hold back a laugh. Even as organized as Jenna is, this is definitely not the type of thing she would have written down. "When you were drunk, you told me that the only way I was allowed to come anymore was inside you."

She's dead silent for a minute. "What?" she finally replies, slow and flustered. "N-no way did I say that."

"Oh, but I remember it perfectly." I'm smirking, despite my overwhelming need. I can't resist the chance to mess with her a little. "You interrogated me about how often I masturbate, and then . . ." I repeat her exact words back to her, low and dirty. "All of your orgasms belong to me. Anytime you need to relieve pressure, you're only allowed to use my pussy."

She makes a noise that sounds something like "guh." I can just picture the pink tint spreading over her cheeks.

I press harder. "I did exactly what you told me, Jenna. I haven't touched myself since. I can't wait until you're ovulating again—I need you so bad it hurts." I don't have to fake the note of desperation in my voice.

An audible swallow. "I . . ." She pauses, and it sounds like she's wavering.

"Please." I'm half-hard just talking to her, anticipating her answer. Hoping for a yes, and *soon*.

"I'm free tonight." Her words rush out. "Come to my place whenever you're done with work. I'll be there."

Thank God. "Absolutely," I purr, pleased to have seduced her.

I hang up and try to force my attention back to my computer. Now I just have to hold on for the rest of the workday . . .

Shit.

• • •

As soon as five o'clock hits, I jump in my car and rush over to Jenna's apartment. I hope to Christ I don't get pulled over for speeding, because I don't want to explain the huge bulge in my pants to a cop. The need to see Jenna, to touch her and smell her, is overpowering. I'm almost embarrassed at the way my heart races as I knock on her door.

It's just sex, for God's sake—it's not like I've never been horny before. But Jenna isn't just any woman.

Then she opens the door and desire obliterates all other thoughts.

She's in her bathrobe. Her indecently short bathrobe that just barely covers her ass, leaving her long, shapely legs and creamy cleavage exposed. Her hair curls at the ends in loose, wet tendrils, and her cheeks are pink. I can smell her flowery shampoo.

Freshly showered. There's nothing I want more than to get her dirty again.

Sweeping her into a breathless kiss, I spin her around and close the door by shoving her against it.

"Well, hello to you too." She chuckles, but her voice dissolves into a moan as I yank the belt of her robe and it falls open, revealing the feast I've been starving for. I bite and suck at her neck, her breasts, gradually dropping to my knees as I kiss my way down. God, she's so warm and soft, and I can't get enough of the little noises she makes.

"Hi, Jenna." My mouth trails down her belly, lower.

"I thought this was about you?" Her hands roam through my hair and her eyes are filled with questions.

I stop just before I devour her pussy right then and there. "It's always going to be about you too . . . and when it's about you, trust me, that makes me very happy."

She squirms to shed her robe completely, and it falls to the floor in a heap. "On the couch," she gasps.

I was ready to devour her right here on the spot. But the couch sounds good too—I can lay her down there. I back off just enough to let her walk past.

She lies back and I kneel between her thighs, shivering when she starts tearing at my zipper. I'm so eager and pent up, I'm already dripping for her. She pulls my cock out and wraps her legs around my back, urging me forward.

"Already? You sure?" I ask.

"Yes." She moans, rubbing her wet center along the underside of my cock.

I slide in, unable to hold back the groan that rumbles in my throat. She sighs in satisfaction, like she's been waiting for this too. Has she gotten any release since last time either? I don't know which is hotter . . . the idea that she controlled herself for me, or the idea that she didn't.

I start thrusting and grin when I immediately find the angle that turns her mewls to screams. Never let it be said that I've lost my touch. Picking up the pace, I pinch and roll her nipples between my fingers, wishing I could crane my head low enough to taste them too.

"Oh fuck, *harder*," she moans.

I obey with enthusiasm but it's been too long; the urge to come is already creeping up on me. My balls start to draw up tight. "Damn," I pant, "I'm getting close."

Her legs yank me in even deeper. "It's okay. Keep going."

"But if I don't slow down, I'm gonna . . ."

Her eyes burn into mine. "Remember what I told

you. Use me for relief. Just let go and give me everything."

I refuse to take my pleasure before she's finished at least once. *Fuck that.* My cock throbs and I bite my lip, stifling a groan at how tight and hot she feels around me.

But there's no way I'm finishing before her. Not a chance in hell.

I pull out and immediately drop to my knees to admire the mouthwatering sight of her wet, flushed pussy lips, slick with her arousal. Her swollen nub pokes out of its sheath, begging for me.

"What are you . . . ," she says, but then I give her neglected clit a long lick. "Oh . . ."

She gasps and her thighs tremble around my head. *Yes . . .*

I taste her again and again, and when she whimpers, I decide that's more than enough teasing and dive in in earnest, rapidly moving my tongue against her clit. Her fingers tangle in my hair, pulling me even closer. She bucks hard into the stimulation, twitching up against my grip on her soft hips.

"Emmett . . ." She groans, and her knees suddenly lock and her trembling ramps up into violent quaking. I hold on tight and keep licking while she shudders apart under my hands.

She slumps back on the couch, panting. I climb up beside her for a kiss, hoping she can taste herself on my lips.

"Need to come now," I growl.

"Yes, inside me." Jenna pulls me close again. Wrapping her fist around my swollen shaft, she guides me to her still-pulsing core and I sink inside.

This woman is going to kill me—and I'm going to enjoy every second of the fall. I can't stop.

She's so tight, so warm, and I'm beyond the point of return. Pumping my hips, I tip helplessly over the edge, spilling pulse after pulse inside her. Her legs hold me close until the last aftershocks fade.

"Damn, that was . . . intense," she says, breathing hard. "Maybe I should keep you pent-up more often."

I let out a half laugh, half groan. "Please don't. These

past two weeks have sucked royally."

I realize that while my statement was true, it's not just because of the lack of sex. It's sucked not spending time with Jenna.

"I'm only teasing you, big boy."

"Evil woman." I bend close and she opens her mouth to me. We share a slow, lazy kiss.

For a while we just sit there on the couch and bask in the afterglow, our arms and legs tangled together, her head on my shoulder. I realize that my earlier hunger wasn't only from a lack of orgasms . . . I've missed this too. Just being near her.

On impulse, I ask, "Would you be interested in going to my cousin Mike's wedding with me next week?"

She doesn't move. Her expression barely changes, but I can feel her close off. "Why?" she asks.

I make a vague noise. "Just a thought. He and Sheila will expect me to bring a date, and I hadn't planned on it initially, but it sounds better than going alone."

Jenna sits up, moving away from me. "I can't be your date to anything because we're not dating. That wasn't part of our deal."

I hold up a hand. "You're right. We're not dating. But trust me when I say it won't be a big deal. My family is used to me bringing a woman around once and *only* once. They'll be perfectly nice, but nobody will get attached or ask awkward questions. No interrogations, no weird expectations, only polite small talk. It'll be like we're just friends." Even friendship is slightly dangerous territory, but hopefully Jenna will still be more receptive to that than the alternative.

She sighs with an odd sort of sad skepticism. "I believe you, but still . . ."

"Please? Come hang out with me so I'm not bored out of my fucking mind," I say in my sweetest tone.

She chews her lip, her gaze downcast, then looks back up at me. "What's in it for me?"

Good, we're getting somewhere. I rub my chin in thought. "I'll . . . give you my slice of wedding cake?"

She snorts with a deadpan expression. "I'm not a

college student anymore. It's been a while since free food was enough to get me to go somewhere I didn't want to go."

"Fine. You drive a hard bargain, Miss Porter. How about, I'll do that thing I did last time that made you scream?" I smirk.

She averts her gaze, her cheeks pink, holding back a smile of her own. "Oh my God, never mention that again. That was embarrassing."

"It was fucking hot." I flash a grin.

"Oh, shut your gross, horndog mouth." She pushes my face away, but she's also laughing, so I count that as points in my favor. "Fine, fine, you win. I'll go with you."

• • •

At the wedding reception the next week, I chill by the open bar, drinking a dry martini and watching Jenna dance a slow, shuffling two-step with Mike's ancient father. She laughs and her nose crinkles. Hah . . . Uncle Kurt must have told one of his famous so-bad-it's-good jokes.

My younger brother, Jake, slides up to the rail beside

me with a smug look, like he thinks he knows something I don't. "So, you and Jenna, huh?"

The slight smile I didn't even know I was wearing slips off. "What about it?"

"Nothing," he says in a tone that means *everything*. He turns to the bartender. "Hey, can I get what he's having? Thanks."

"Where's Heather?" I ask. *You know, your infant daughter who you should go play with instead of bothering me about Jenna?*

"With Nicole, don't worry." He takes an infuriatingly nonchalant sip of his martini.

Nearby, my older sister, Aubrey, peels off from her husband and their three young children and walks over with baby Dustin asleep in her arms. She beams at me. "You guys are talking about Jenna? Isn't she the greatest?"

Narrowing my eyes, I look back and forth between them with the deepest suspicion. "This is a conspiracy, isn't it? What are you guys plotting?"

Jake raises his palms. "No plotting here."

"Don't try to deny it," I reply. "Just skip to the part where you tell me what you're up to."

"We like Jenna. That's all." Aubrey sways slightly, rocking her son despite the fact that he's clearly already dead to the world. "During the ceremony, when Kimberly started throwing a tantrum? Jenna offered to hold Dustin so I could focus on getting her to cool her jets. Usually, he's scared of new people, but he couldn't have been happier. Just giggling up a storm, babbling and cooing and reaching out to touch her face . . ."

"I know, Aubrey," I say as patiently as I can, which isn't very. "I was sitting right next to you two. I saw the whole thing. And I already knew she loves babies." It's sort of the whole reason that we're doing whatever this is . . . but I certainly don't tell either of them that. It's not at all surprising that Jenna is a natural mother. "So, what's your point?"

Aubrey fixes me with one of her patented *what are you, stupid?* big-sister looks. "My point is that she's super sweet."

"Uh, I agree?" I reply cautiously. Where are they

going with all this?

"She's wicked smart too," Jake says. "I was just talking to her earlier about small-business taxes. Do you know if she takes any accounting work? We could really use a hand with that down at the store."

I shrug. "Probably not. She owns her own business, in antiques."

"Darn. Anyway, we both think you gotta lock this girl down." Jake raises his eyebrows at me. "She's the one, dude."

Are you two shitting me right now? I put down my drink with a sharp clack. "You just met the woman a few hours ago. How the . . ." I glance at the still-sleeping baby whose tousled head lies cradled on Aubrey's shoulder. ". . . heck do you know anything?"

"Oh, we can tell a good catch when we see one. She's totally different from the women you usually date. No offense, but your taste has gotten way better, little bro." Aubrey smirks. "And we'd have to be blind to miss the way you look at her."

I pinch the bridge of my nose. The thing is, I can't be

too pissed because they're absolutely right. Jenna really is amazing—the total package—and she fits right in with my family. But Aubrey and Jake don't know the reasons why dating her wouldn't work, and I can't explain it to them. Jenna and I have to stick to the deal we agreed upon when we started this thing. I need to focus one hundred percent on running the company, and she said her life plan doesn't have any room for a relationship either. No boyfriend, no husband, no man who offers anything more than being a sperm donor.

"She's not interested in getting serious," I finally grumble, my stomach feeling a little sour. I drain the last of my martini and push the glass across the bar.

Aubrey immediately leaps for the jugular. "She said that? You've asked her specifically?"

Shit, I've made a mistake. I shouldn't have let even that tiny nugget of information slip. "Yes," I say, my reply clipped and flat.

"So, you *want* to get serious with her?" Jake asks.

"No. We talked about relationship boundaries like a couple of mature goddamned adults, and the subject came up." Dustin stirs, and I force myself to calm down and lower my voice. "It's complicated, okay? Please just drop it."

Aubrey and Jake share a long look. Then Jake says, "All right, dude. Sorry."

"Go on and enjoy the party. I think she's free now." Aubrey points across the reception hall to the dance floor, where Jenna is waving good-bye to a middle-aged woman I don't know. One of the bride's relatives, maybe. I guess the Smith clan aren't the only ones smitten with her.

"Sure, I'll go dance with her." The prospect lightens the crappy mood that Aubrey and Jake put me in with all their relationship talk. As long as I'm here, I may as well enjoy a dance or two—there's no harm in that, right? "See you guys later."

I order a Mai Tai and weave my way through the crowd to the table where Jenna has just taken a seat. "Here," I say, offering the cocktail. "All danced out already?"

She looks beautiful tonight. In a strapless lavender gown with her long hair twisted into some elegant knot at the nape of her neck, she's stunning. Best of all? She's wearing that lipstick I love—the bright shade that makes the color in her cheeks pop too.

"Nah, just wanted a quick break." She takes a long drink. She relaxed her stance on drinking after I told her many babies were convinced under the influence. "Mmm . . . that's really tasty. Thank you."

I sit with her while she sips until the band changes to a good song, then I stand up and offer my hand. "Care to dance?"

She hops to her feet and sets her half-empty glass aside. "I'd love to."

As we stroll onto the dance floor, I ask, "Are you having fun?"

"Yes, actually. Everyone's been so friendly." Then her smile turns into something much less innocent. "But I'm looking forward to the end of the night."

Oh . . . when we'll go back to our shared hotel room. Which has only one bed.

I grin back at her and agree with a kiss.

Chapter Thirteen

Jenna

As soon as our hotel room door swings shut behind us, we crash together in a desperate fever of lust. Emmett's body, his desire, is hard against my belly. It makes my knees weak.

We tear at each other's clothes in a frenzy, racing for the primal contact of skin on skin. My dress is unzipped and it falls to a puddle at my feet. Next, he gets my bra off and flings it aside. My fingers fumble halfway down his shirt buttons and pause at the sultry caress of his mouth on my sensitive breasts.

"Emmett . . ." I groan, pushing my fingers into his hair.

His arm wraps around my waist to pull me against him. His bulge presses into my stomach, so hot and hard it feels like it could burn straight through my panties to where I want it most. I shiver and try to rock against it but his grip tightens, holding my hips steady.

"Not yet. You get your turn first."

I've forgotten how insistent he is about my orgasms

coming before his. It seems like an archaic, old-fashioned tradition, but in this moment, I'm totally on board.

His fingers slip between my legs, pushing aside my damp panties. His middle and index fingers slide over my clit a few times, teasing a needy noise out of me before delving lower and pushing inside. They crook up, right into my G-spot, and my knees buckle.

"Emmett," I plead, my voice unrecognizable, husky and almost pained with need. His fingertips work my G-spot while the heel of his hand grinds against my clit. I can't handle it. This is way too much and I want more. Never before has sex been like this. Never before have *I* been like this, so wanton. "Inside me . . . Right the fuck now."

He makes a grunt of need, and the sound hits me straight in the chest.

"Emm . . . please." I'm already barely coherent, but he understands.

"You sure you're ready? Anything for you." With a growl of lust and pride, he yanks my panties down my legs and picks me up like I weigh nothing.

Shit.

Then, bracing me against the wall, he unzips his pants, finally freeing his cock, and pushes inside. It's no small effort either. In this position, with my legs almost closed, he works his thick cock back and forth through my labia until he's coated in my juices before spearing me deeply. I can feel him everywhere.

I bite my lip so hard to stifle my scream, it bruises. *Oh yes*, I've been anticipating this all day, ever since we drove out here. Emmett lifts me, and I cross my ankles behind his back and squeeze eagerly, my vaginal muscles tightening around him.

Holding us chest to chest, his hands groping my ass, he slowly eases himself in to the hilt and just as slowly withdraws until only the very tip of his cock remains.

All of me feels the loss of him. I'm desperate to feel his skin on mine, filling me.

"Please ... please ..." Hot all over, I wriggle and buck, but I can't move much when I'm pinned between him and the wall like this. *Come on, you clit-tease, I've waited long enough.*

"Fuck." He groans. "You feel so perfect."

I buck against him again and Emmett makes a satisfyingly needy sound, but more importantly, he keeps up with those infuriatingly gentle rolls of his hips. The head of his cock brushes my G-spot and I moan, begging.

"There," he whispers and suddenly slams into me at the exact perfect angle, tearing my first unrestrained cry from my throat.

He smothers my outburst with a rough kiss, nothing more than a messy, hungry clash of lips and tongue. Now his thrusts come hard and fast and, *oh my sweet fucking God*, it's everything I've ever wanted, my clit rubbing against his pelvic bone and his cock pounding my G-spot like he was custom-made for my pussy.

How the hell does he do this to me? How can he strip away my inhibitions, reduce me to a horny mess, rule my world with a mere touch? What is this wild magic that lets us click and work together so exquisitely, wringing the pleasure from each other's bodies? It feels like his hands are everywhere, caressing and groping, his fingers digging into my hips while his hot, wet mouth spreads sloppy kisses and bites all over my neck. He wakes my whole body until my head is swimming and every nerve sparks all at once.

This isn't just baby-making anymore. Deep down, I know it hasn't been for a long time. The fire that consumes us every time we meet has nothing to do with procreation and everything to do with pure chemical lust. I shouldn't love it so much, but holy hell, I couldn't fight this feeling even if I wanted to. And I definitely don't want to. He's so perfect. So hot. So sexy. How will I ever get enough?

"Don't stop," I demand, panting. "Please don't fucking stop. *Oh God*, right there . . ."

"You feel so fucking good." Emmett groans again and the sound vibrates through me.

I squeeze my eyes shut and bury my face in his throat, gasping for breath as my release slams through me with a force that leaves me quivering, quaking, trembling in his arms.

Emmett pulls back enough to meet my eyes. "You okay? You're shaking."

I swallow and nod. "Yes."

"You had enough?" His voice is tight.

"You haven't come yet." Why on earth would he want to stop?

"That doesn't matter. Seriously. If you're tired, or . . ."

I have no idea why my entire body is trembling. But I really don't care. My brain is screaming at me not to stop—never to stop—and the desire to watch him lose control is even more intense. "I want you to come. And I'm not stopping until you do."

Still inside me, he carries me to the bed. I'm grateful; my legs have turned to jelly and I'm not sure I wouldn't just fall flat on my face. Only after he's laid me down does he start moving again, thrusting in long, deep strokes. With one hand pinned above my head in his large palm, he places my other between the apex of my thighs.

"Touch yourself. Make yourself come for me," he says.

I obey, rubbing gentle circles against my clit with my

index finger, even though I'm sure I won't be able to come again. But soon, my body is calling my bluff and I'm building toward climax.

"Yes, yes, yes," I pant.

He continues those deep, steady thrusts, his gaze wandering lower to watch me touch myself. "God, that's a fucking sexy view."

At the sound of his deep, drugged voice, I lose it, my inner muscles pulsing wildly around him, milking him as I climax.

"That's it. Fuck. Jesus. Jenna . . ." Emmett finally losing control is the most beautiful sound I've ever heard. With jerky movements, he finally comes inside me with a groan.

After, he gently withdraws and lays down beside me, gathering me close. "Shit. That was . . ."

"Amazing," I finish for him.

Spent, all I can do is lie there while I float back down from heaven. Our eyes meet and we share a sated smile.

The afterglow is always so wonderful . . . and so

dangerous. In the past, I've been far too tempted to stay with him, to bask in comfort until I fall asleep and then wake up beside him. To breathe in his scent, to enjoy the feel of his firm, muscled chest under me, and this time, I can't sneak away. Tonight, there's no way to get out of sharing the same bed. Which isn't great for my mental health, I decide.

"Um . . ." I clear my throat. "You want the shower first?"

He looks confused for a moment at the sudden change of subject, then shrugs. "You can have it."

"No, it's fine, you go. Just let me grab my toiletry bag."

Emmett blinks at me and then rises from the bed.

While he showers, I brush my teeth at the open vanity and try not to think about him being naked and wet less than ten feet from me. Christ, this situation is so awkward. Or maybe he's totally fine and it's just awkward for me because my stupid heart won't shut up. It's talking a mile a minute with every beat it takes.

I like Emmett. I really, *really* like him. And that scares the shit out of me. That wasn't part of the deal. I was supposed to only want his sperm—not *him*.

And the fact is, I'm getting way too close to him. I need to remember that this is only temporary and I absolutely can't get attached. No matter how sexy and fun and dependable he is, or how nicely his family welcomed me today, or how lonely I was before we met, I can't rely on a man like that. In thirty-five years, I've never been able to rely on anyone with a penis. It never works out.

Men are assholes. I need to repeat this to myself a few times for good measure.

Dammit ... Emmett has been nothing short of perfect so far. Like that night I got my period, when I was so drunk and depressed. I didn't even remember asking Emmett not to masturbate, but he took my words seriously anyway. And he always does—he pays attention to what I say and makes a point of listening, really listening, to me. The way he prioritizes me is so damn refreshing compared to how guys have treated me in the past. When he called me at work last week, I wasn't just turned on, I was touched. He was thinking about me in the middle of his workday, and wanted only me.

I mean, I was incredibly turned on too. It was positively heady, having so much sexual power over such an attractive, confident man. A man who could have anyone, but chose me.

With that kind of man, there must be a way to work things out, right?

Stop it. You're doing it again. Men always prove themselves untrustworthy in the end. They always leave you or turn out to be dirtbags ... or both. At least Emmett was up front about his desires—to fuck and have fun and then wave a friendly good-bye once I'm pregnant. I can't confuse this for something it's not.

But, but, but . . . my heart insists.

Our time together has a set expiration date, and even though it will be hard, it's also necessary. For a fleeting moment, the flash of a memory takes hold. I reflect on what my friends told me way back when, that love shows up when you aren't looking for it anymore.

I spit into the sink. "Shut up," I mutter out loud.

A large hand lands on my shoulder, pulling me from my thoughts. "You ready?"

"Huh?" I startle and whirl around. Emmett is standing behind me in his low-hanging pajama pants, bare-chested, his hair tousled and wet. *Yum.* Yes, I'm very ready.

"I said, I'm done. You can have the shower now," he says.

"Oh. Right. Yes, showering." I step toward the bathroom, then hesitate. "Emmett . . . last week, if you wanted relief so badly, why didn't you just jerk off?"

He blinks like he doesn't understand the question. "Because you asked me not to, and I said I wouldn't. A promise is a promise." He pauses, then smiles at me. "If I say I'm going to do something, I mean it. I want to be the kind of man you can rely on . . . you know, since getting you pregnant is a priority for both of us."

My stomach squiggles all too pleasantly. He would put up with such a silly, frustrating demand just for me? "I see. Um . . . thank you," I blurt and hurry into the shower.

I wash my hair for a long time, as if I can massage

the chaos in my head into some kind of coherence, into a resolve to stick to the plan like I know I should. But everything keeps circling around. Like the water rushing down the drain, my thoughts are swirling, making me dizzy with uncertainty.

I emerge in my pajamas, toweling my hair dry, to find Emmett already done with his routine and in bed.

"You coming?" he asks.

"Yeah." Almost cautiously, I climb in and slide under the covers beside him. He's so warm and smells so good.

God, how many years has it been since I've shared a bed with a man? I've been sleeping alone for so long, it should feel foreign, but instead it feels so right. Like coming home. When I inhale the scent of his clean skin, it takes all the stress and worry out of my muscles.

Despite his relaxing presence, though, my anxieties still won't leave me alone. After fifteen minutes of inspecting the wallpaper like there's a magic problem-solving spell hidden in its pattern, I ask, "You asleep yet?"

Emmett's voice in the darkness replies, "Nope."

I turn on the bedside lamp and sit up. "I don't know why I'm not tired yet." We've had a long day—not to mention all the exercise we just got—but somehow I'm wide awake.

He lets out a long, resigned breath through his nose. "Well, me neither, so let's do something."

"We could . . . watch TV?" I frown. The idea sounds boring, even to me.

He rubs his chin for a minute. "Why don't we play a game?"

"Like Monopoly or something?"

"No, I didn't bring any board games. I meant a cheesy high-school game like Truth or Dare, or Never Have I Ever." He waggles his eyebrows. "Or Spin the Bottle."

My body is so sated from the orgasms he just gave me, I don't think I can go again. "I think we've got make-outs covered, thanks." I pat him on the shoulder. "How does Never Have I Ever work?"

"You haven't played it before?" His expression is a

soft mixture of confusion and surprise.

I shrug. "I guess I wasn't invited to those kinds of parties in high school." Or anytime after that, actually.

"The way it works is someone starts with, 'Never have I ever,' and then they say something they've never done, and anyone who *has* done it has to do some kind of penalty action. You take turns going in a circle—or back and forth, since there's only two of us—until somebody has lost three times, which ends the round."

"Sounds pretty simple. So, what will we use for a penalty? I'm guessing it's a drinking game?"

"There's a minibar in here." He points to it. "We can take a drink every time we lose."

I nod. "All right, let's do it."

We gather a small pile of miniature liquor bottles and sit cross-legged on the bed, facing each other. "Flip a coin for first turn?" he asks.

I wave my hand. "Nah, you go first. You know the rules; you can show me how it works."

"Okay." He unscrews a tiny bottle of whiskey. "This one always gets at least a few people in the room. Never have I ever owned a dog or a cat."

"Oh, you poor thing." I take the proffered whiskey and swallow a mouthful, grimacing at the burn. "We had a big old mutt named Heidi. She was so gentle and friendly, Mom let her play with me even when I was hardly more than a toddler." Then I look back up at him. "Wait, you said 'dog or cat' specifically, not 'pet.' Did you have something else?"

"Yeah. In principle, my parents approved of pets as a way for us to learn responsibility."

That attitude seems awfully unsentimental, I can't help thinking. Seeing pets as just teaching tools, not as loving companions? I keep the commentary to myself, though. Maybe we're just different. Maybe Heidi wouldn't have been so crucial to my childhood if I had more human family and friends.

"But Dad was allergic to cats," Emmett continues, "and Mom didn't want anything that made noise or messes, so no dogs or birds either. Aubrey got a turtle, Jake got a hamster, and I got tropical fish."

"What about after you left home?" I ask.

"I've mostly kept to having fish off and on over the years. I've always thought it might be cool to have a dog—to take on hikes, camping, things like that—but I've never had the time to devote all the attention they need, and it would be cruel to get one just to ignore it since I'm at the office so much." He looks pensive, almost brooding for a moment. Then he says, "Anyway, it's your turn now."

"Hmm. Never have I ever . . ." I ponder briefly. "Been outside the United States."

His eyebrows wing up. "What, seriously?"

"Yep. So, did you go abroad on business trips? Or family vacations?"

He shakes his head. "For work, I mostly deal with domestic companies. And my family . . . was never one for doing things together."

"Oh." I study the carpet for a minute, feeling a tiny bit like a jerk. I might have grown up without a father, but I've always been close with Mom. "Then what was the occasion for traveling?"

"After college and before I started at Dad's company, my buddy Jesse and I toured Europe." He takes a swig of vodka, draining half the tiny bottle.

"That's amazing. What was your favorite part?"

"I was probably too young to appreciate the rich history and culture back then, but we backpacked across France and Italy, so I have a lot of good memories. There are so many ancient and beautiful sites; I'd love to go back someday."

I don't know how to respond. *It would be fun to go with you* is totally off-limits, even if I wanted to, which I try to convince myself I don't. So I end up replying, "That sounds really cool. Your turn again."

"I guess it is, huh?" He pauses to stretch, his back popping quietly. "Okay. Never have I ever ... seen *Titanic.*"

"Swing and a miss," I reply cheerfully. "I never saw that movie either." Which means no booze for me, at least until Emmett's next turn.

He raises his arms like he's begging the ceiling for mercy. "Oh, come on. Fine. Give me your best shot."

"Never have I ever eaten sushi." I stick the very tip of my tongue out to tease him. I think the liquor is already going to my head.

"No way." He gapes at me. "Now you're just fucking with me. Seriously, never? Okay, next time we go out, I'm taking you to my favorite sushi bar."

"Deal." I've given up trying to stop him inviting me on date-like activities. And to be honest . . . I don't want to stop. I like hanging out together too much. Grinning at him, I tease, "Don't forget your drink."

"Yeah, yeah." He slugs back the remaining vodka and tosses the empty bottle in the trash. "In your defense, I didn't develop a taste for sushi until I was almost thirty."

"So, there's still time for me?"

"Yes, young grasshopper. Now, my turn again." He gives me an evil smirk. "You're a literary type, so . . . never have I ever tried to write a novel."

I glare at him and push at his firm bicep. "Hey, that's

playing dirty."

He spreads his hands in a gesture of self-defense. "That's how the game works, baby. Feel free to use every fact you know about me too. So, what was your novel about and where can I buy it?"

"It was a children's book, and you can't. I abandoned it when I realized it sucked." I drain my whiskey and toss the bottle.

He gives me a sympathetic look. "I'm sure you were just being too hard on yourself."

"No, the idea really was dumb." I shake my head with a wry laugh. "Back to the game. Since you're pulling out all the stops here, never have I ever slept with a woman."

"Fuck." He unscrews another bottle of vodka and takes a drink. "You're kicking my ass here."

"Quit whining, you've only drunk one more time than me. And what, are you saying I'm boring? Because there's too many things I haven't done?" I pretend to pout.

"I would never." He puts his hand right over my heart, his features softening. "I just need to find the right questions to ask." Then he flashes me a smile. "If I didn't know better, I'd think you're trying to get me drunk to take advantage of me."

"Mr. Booty Call, I can take advantage of you whenever I want. I don't need help from alcohol." I give him a playful, feather-light punch in the shoulder.

"You just want me for my cum."

It's the stupidest joke, and I haven't drunk nearly enough to get this goofy yet, but I can't stop giggling until I'm slumped on the bed with aching sides.

He laughs too and leans against the headboard with his vodka. "Enjoy your victory while it lasts. I'll beat you next round."

We play for another hour, forgetting about the liquor, but just to continue the conversation. The rest of his questions all zero in on me like he's known me forever, and I end up only one point behind him. If my brain weren't so fuzzy from the alcohol, I might find it strange that two people well into their thirties needed to use the guise of a drinking game to learn more about each other, but I try not to focus on things like that with Emmett. I try to remind myself to just enjoy the here and now.

We snuggle under the covers again, and this time, my tension has vanished. I should be more distressed by exactly how much I like sharing a bed with Emmett. But I can't bring myself to be upset when I'm cuddled up to him like this, safe in his warm, strong arms.

I promise myself that I'll freak out in the morning, and drift off into a peaceful sleep.

Chapter Fourteen

Emmett

I wake to the unwelcome racket of someone knocking energetically on the door. Jenna sits up beside me, blinking blearily, her hair disheveled in an adorable way that makes me want to memorize how she looks right now.

"Huh?" she mumbles.

I couldn't agree more. At another flurry of brisk knocks, I groan aloud, rubbing the sleep out of my eyes. "Coming, coming. Just a damn minute."

I trudge over and open the door to Aubrey, bright-eyed and bushy-tailed. She gives the both of us a sappy smile, as if to coo, *Aww, how cute.* "Good morning, you two," she chirps.

I almost growl *What do you want?* and immediately wonder why I'm in such a shitty mood today. I manage a reasonably friendly sounding "What's up?" instead.

"The rest of the family was thinking about going out for brunch before everyone heads back home," Aubrey says. "Want to join us?"

Brunch? What time is it? I squint at the clock. Whoa, it's almost ten thirty. I was sleeping so deeply, I didn't even hear my alarm. Good thing Aubrey came by or we'd miss our checkout time.

Jenna, still in her pajamas, pads up behind me. "I'm up for it if you are, Emmett."

The prospect of one last hangout with my family should sound wonderful, but for some reason, I'd rather eat a bug than have brunch while my family coos all over Jenna. I shake my head. "I'm afraid we should leave soon."

"Leave? Already?" Aubrey protests. "But—"

"I'm sorry," I say quickly, interrupting her. "I'm worried about how things are going back at the office."

Jenna frowns, clearly disappointed, but nods in acceptance. She knows the business world never rests.

"I'm sure they can survive a few more hours without you. You won't get back to the city until afternoon anyway, so why not just take the whole day off?" Aubrey argues.

"I'm telling you I can't," I snap. Shit, that came out way harsher than I intended. I try to soften my tone with a joke. "Wish I could, but you know what Dad always said about upper management . . . couldn't pour sand out of a boot with instructions written on the heel."

"All right, if you insist." Aubrey's reply is slow and doubtful. "At least grab some of the free breakfast downstairs. It's been picked over pretty thoroughly, but I think I saw some muffins and yogurt left."

"We'll do that." I reach for the doorknob.

Aubrey adds, "It's been great seeing you. Hopefully we can do it again soon . . . and feel free to bring Jenna with you." She winks.

I grit my teeth. "Definitely. I'll call you." I shut the door before she can say anything else.

I'm acting like a total dick. I'll have to apologize later or face my sister's patented cold shoulder. I should probably apologize to Jenna too for depriving her of a nice brunch; she couldn't exactly stay without me, since I'm her ride. But right now, all I can focus on is the desperate need to get the hell out of here.

I have no idea why I'm so edgy. In the light of day, it all seems suddenly overwhelming—how great spending time with Jenna has been, how much my whole family loves her, how intense last night was, everything about this trip. Which doesn't make any sense . . . those should have all been good things. And they were at the time, but now they scrape and scratch at me like sandpaper.

We shower in a hurry and get dressed, pack our suitcases, eat quickly and quietly, and are soon on our way. In the car, Jenna shoots me quick sidelong glances every few minutes, like she's trying to keep an eye on a wild animal without provoking it.

After almost half an hour, she finally asks, "Did I . . . do something wrong?"

Guilt twinges in my stomach. Shit, I've freaked her out. I shouldn't let my inexplicable grouchiness poison the air like that. "No, you're fine," I quickly reassure her. "I just need to get back to the city."

"I see," she says softly. Then she turns away to look out the passenger window.

We drive on in silence so tense it hurts, buildings and

trees and fields whipping past. *Goddammit.* My hands clench white-knuckled on the steering wheel. I practically chewed off my own leg to get away from the party, but now that we're away, something in me regrets it. Why am I acting like this—*feeling* like this? Why can't I figure out what I want?

Well . . . I steal a glance at Jenna. I know at least one thing I want. But I can't have it. That wasn't our deal.

I do my best to remind myself that as fun as Jenna is, all of this is only temporary. Our lives and goals are way too different. We can't change just because we've had a few weeks of fun. It's impossible.

But right now, for the life of me, I can't remember exactly *why* it's impossible.

Jenna shifts uncomfortably in her seat. "Um . . . your family is great."

It's obvious she's trying to make conversation, and that I need to throw her a bone or else this suffocating atmosphere might kill us. But it's hard when my family's reaction to her is part of what's bothering me.

"Yeah, they are." My voice comes out brusquer than I intended, and I clear my throat. "I mean, my parents were totally dysfunctional, but as adults, my brother, sister, and I are really close."

And both of them are married, in love, with kids. The goddamn poster children for wedded bliss. Which makes me wonder, for the thousandth time, just what the hell went wrong with me.

"Listen," Jenna says, and her firm tone makes me look at her—and then right back to the road because I can't deal with her penetrating gaze. "You've been acting weird ever since we got up this morning. Are you okay? Do you still want to do this?"

"Of course I do." The answer leaps from my mouth whip-quick. I've never wanted anything more. Then I catch myself. I can't be too eager, too raw with her. Trying to recover, to convince myself as much as her, I quip, "Fuck a gorgeous woman for fun? What man wouldn't be interested in that? I don't even have to buy you dinner first. Well, I offer to take you to dinner most times, at least."

Her lovely features turn down subtly. She swallows,

opens and closes her mouth, then mutters, "Right. Okay. Just wanted to make sure."

Her strained expression tightens further. She's blinking slightly faster than before. Even with my focus on the road, I can tell she's upset, and the guilty knowledge knifes deep into my gut.

Fuck, I didn't want to hurt her. That's the last thing I would ever want. But I don't even understand what I said wrong. From the moment we met, she's been dead set on keeping things temporary, casual, no strings attached. A transaction with a strict expiration date, not a relationship. So, isn't a fuck buddy exactly what she was after?

"I didn't mean it like that," I say, fumbling, hating that I've upset her.

"It's fine. You didn't say anything wrong." Jenna's voice is low, somehow sharp and thick at the same time. She's looking away from me again, out the window.

I wish I could at least see her face to get a hint of her feelings. I'm blundering around in the dark here, so I start rambling. "I mean, it's not that I don't like buying you dinner. I actually really enjoy—"

What the fuck? Of all the words in the English language I could have said, why did my useless brain pick something so stupid? I just want to touch her, but my hands are stuck and I feel like I can't.

She mercifully cuts me off. "I said it's fine. We're still on for next week, right?"

"Yeah," I grumble. It's clearly not fine. But what's equally clear is that Jenna doesn't want to discuss it anymore. If she says she's okay, what more can I do other than drop it? And a cowardly, shameful part of me is grateful for the reprieve, because prying into her feelings would mean prying into my own too.

I check the car clock. We still have an hour and a half until we're back in the city and I can drop her off. Fuck, this is going to be a long, awkward drive home.

Despite how everything suddenly went to hell today . . . I almost don't even want to go back to that dark, cold penthouse of mine, when I know Jenna won't be there with me.

Chapter Fifteen

Jenna

It's time. Standing in front of my bathroom sink after a long day at work, I wince and inject my second trigger shot. Starting in twenty-four hours, I'll need to fuck Emmett as much as humanly possible. I already scheduled a meeting with him but I'm feeling antsy, so I decide to triple-check.

As I reach for my phone, though, it rings on its own. A call from Emmett. Surprised, I pick up and say, "Hello?"

"Hi, Jenna. I'm afraid something's come up at work."

My heart jumps into my throat. "What? What do you mean?"

"I have to go on a last-minute business trip to New York. I fly out tomorrow at noon and come back in three days."

"But that's exactly when I'm ovulating." I don't believe this. He can't just skip town now.

He sighs in a rush of static. "I know. I'm really sorry.

I called you as soon as I could get a moment away. We only realized just this afternoon that there was a problem with one of our distributors, and I have to go straighten it out in person."

"Shit," I grumble. I try to think of a way around this but can't come up with anything.

He's been acting strange ever since the wedding. Well, that's not true. The wedding, the reception, and our evening in the hotel were all perfect. The weirdness started on the drive back to the city. Maybe this business trip is just a fabrication. Maybe he doesn't want to see me anymore.

I'm trying not to panic, but I can hear my pulse pounding in my ears as I pace. My throat is dry. *It can't all have been for nothing this month*, I think as I rub my fingers against my temples.

After a minute of silence as I frantically pace around my apartment, he says, "Maybe you could come with me?"

I stop wearing a hole in the carpet. "To New York?"

"Yeah, why not? I'd pay for the flight and hotel and

everything, since I'm putting you in a tight spot."

I chew on my lip, relief rushing through me at the knowledge that he's not trying to get out of our arrangement after all. "I don't know. I can't just suddenly close my store like that," I reluctantly argue.

"Are you the only staff member or something?" he asks.

"No, I have an assistant, but—"

"Is he trustworthy?"

"She's a she, and yes, but—"

"Well, there you go. Isn't this kind of thing that assistants are for?"

"It's not exactly standard procedure to ask people to shoulder extra duties so their bosses can go get laid," I say dryly.

"You know what I meant. She can cover for you a few days without burning the place down."

I take a moment to think. But apparently I'm quiet for too long.

"So, what do you say?" he says. "It could be fun. I'd have to be in boring meetings for most of the day, but we could hang out after. Drinking, dancing, fine dining, whatever you want to do." His voice takes on that sultry tone I find so hard to resist. "Of course, at night I'll be all yours."

The temptation to spend so much time with Emmett—not to mention avoid wasting this month's ovulation—is just too strong. "Okay," I finally reply, rationalizing that it's not like there will be too many customers for Britt to manage solo.

"Great," he says with genuine enthusiasm. "I'll pick you up tomorrow morning at nine."

"See you then. 'Bye." I hang up, letting out a sigh.

I've tried to pretend that the day after Mike's wedding never happened, but in moments when I'm not busy or guarded enough, it still finds its way under my skin to gnaw at me. Emmett's comment about me being a quick-and-easy fling really stung. Which just made me even more confused and frustrated, because I shouldn't have any feelings about this situation to hurt. Yet there I sat, staring out the car window with a knot in my throat that I still can't explain, let alone forget.

Emmett hasn't brought it up, so I can't tell if he forgot about that weird, painful interlude . . . or he's been playing along with my charade of uncomplicated contentment. Either way *should* be good enough for me, but of course I'm still wondering what he's thinking, because my heart is an asshole who enjoys pain and can't follow the simplest fucking instructions.

And yet I can't stay away from him. I don't even want to. I swore that I'd never be the kind of woman who needs a man. But somehow, despite my best efforts, here I am . . . unable to escape his gravitational pull.

I start packing a suitcase, already abuzz with anticipation for three solid days of Emmett.

• • •

We touch down on the LaGuardia tarmac mid-afternoon and arrive at our hotel on the Upper East Side an hour later. When we see our room, I'm almost afraid to touch anything. The luxuriously decorated suite boasts a balcony offering a gorgeous view of the city skyline, a huge marble-floored bathroom with a Jacuzzi tub, and a plush king-sized bed bearing a small box of truffles on each pillow. I wander around, taking it all in, while Emmett tips the bellboy who brought up our bags and sends him back downstairs.

Without taking off his suit jacket or shoes, Emmett moves my suitcase to the foot of the bed, leaving his own suitcase by the coat rack. "I'll be in meetings until five," he explains, "so I'm afraid you'll be on your own during the day, but we can do whatever we want at night. I'll be back in a couple of hours. Will you be okay? I feel like a dick for leaving you."

I wave him off. "Don't. I'll be fine. I may take a nap, and a bubble bath in that tub sounds amazing. You don't need to worry. I'll be ready for dinner when you get back."

"I'm not worried. I know you're a big girl, Jenna. I just don't like abandoning you. I hear the hotel has an excellent spa." His mouth quirks. "Or there's the New York Public Library, the museum . . ."

"Of course. You know me too well." I chuckle.

"I try my best." He leans in, hesitates, and bends

down to pick up his briefcase. "Well, I've got to run. I'll be back as soon as I can get away, and then let's decide where to go for dinner."

The door closes behind him, leaving me alone and unsettled. Did he just stop himself from kissing me goodbye? God, that doesn't help my state of mind. I'm overthinking this; my mind is playing tricks on me and my heart isn't getting the message. A trip to the library sounds like just what I need . . . silence, solitude, and the friendly company of books will clear my head.

After I freshen up, I call a taxi to drop me off near Bryant Park. I walk across the manicured grass, between the great stone lions guarding the New York Public Library, and into a breathtaking literary cathedral. The scent of old paper embraces me. Room upon room and shelves upon shelves of books stretch out on all sides. For a long while, I just wander the stacks and reading rooms in peaceful awe, admiring the beautiful architecture and the combined wisdom of centuries. I could spend the rest of my life reading here and never finish even half their collection. It's incredible, and I'm at a loss about where to start.

I decide to just stroll around the literary fiction section and pick up whatever catches my eye. With relish, I read snippets from all the new titles I've heard good reviews for, but haven't gotten around to evaluating for myself.

After a while, though, I realize I'm still antsy, which in turn frustrates me. I have hours to kill in one of the world's grandest libraries, dammit—I should feel like a kid in a candy store. But my thoughts keep turning back to Emmett, especially that moment in our hotel room earlier, when he stopped himself from kissing me.

It only heightens the anxiety that was already building around our relationship. What do I feel for him, and is it the same as he feels for me?

I shake my head. No . . . it doesn't matter. Our lives don't fit together, period, end of story. Acknowledging this rift out loud would, at best, make it impossible to go on without making changes that I'm not ready for. At worst, it would bring everything crashing down, and drive away the man I'm finding it harder and harder to imagine my days without.

But that awareness of how precarious our situation is

only lends a desperate edge to my craving. I find myself glancing away from the book in my hand and to my watch every twenty minutes or so, looking forward to the time I'll have him all to myself again.

On a mission, I put the book back into its rightful place and turn to leave. I've decided that when he comes back to our hotel room, I want him to find me waiting there.

• • •

Arching up off the mattress, my feet braced on Emmett's sturdy shoulders, I squirm and moan for more as his tongue flickers over my clit and his skilled fingers massage tirelessly inside me. What we're doing doesn't make sense. Oral sex won't accomplish the reason we started meeting up in the first place. But neither of us comments on that obvious truth. We're just enjoying ourselves ... and dancing around the elephant in the room, trying not to burst this bubble of unspoken tension.

At least, that's why *I'm* keeping my mouth shut. But while it might just be my oversexed imagination, I sense that he's doing the same.

When we got back to the hotel room after dinner, I pounced on him, yanking his pants down and hungrily sucking him off until he almost emptied himself into my mouth.

Only Emmett thought to stop us, to make sure he ejaculated inside me. And, boy, did he. The memory of his deep groan is enough to send me hurtling to the edge.

I throw my head back with a wild cry. Despite everything, despite myself, my time with Emmett is still a blessed vacation from my life. His touch transforms me into a wanton, greedy creature of desire. Just a female animal in heat with no past or future, no worries or shame or overthinking, no bullshit about work . . . just the pure, simple pleasure of the moment. With a desperate moan, I tip over the edge, my body spasming around his fingers in wave after blissful wave.

"So beautiful when you come," he says.

Emmett rises and situates us in the bed together. We lie down on our sides, facing each other.

We share a leisurely, sated kiss, enjoying the sensation of our lips lightly brushing. We part . . . and for a moment, time pauses while our gazes linger on each other. He brushes a stray hair from my face with a smile that skewers my heart.

Emmett looks so tender, I almost tell him how much he means to me. But no . . . that wouldn't do anyone any good. He made his feelings clear from day one. He doesn't have the time or desire for a girlfriend, let alone a family. I shove away the terrible, foolish idea, and it feels like I'm ripping away something inside me along with it.

We turn off the bedside lamps and snuggle down under the covers together. I curl up with my head on his chest, basking in his warmth and the sense of security he always radiates.

I had hotly anticipated three nights of sex with Emmett. What I didn't count on was the fact that I'd spend those nights sleeping in his arms too. Just like the wedding we went to, I love it . . . and hate it. I crave this intimacy so badly, despite knowing that it's a stupid impulse to give in to if I want to avoid getting attached. But maybe it's too late. Maybe I'm already attached, and the best I can do now is let myself enjoy this while it lasts.

His hand gently stroking my hair soothes the ache in my chest. But I know that it isn't gone, only retreated, waiting for the next time I'm alone with my thoughts.

I clench my eyes shut, as if I could block out the truth along with my tears, and let his heartbeat lull me to sleep.

Chapter Sixteen

Emmett

It's the last full day of our New York trip, and I'm torn. On the one hand, I'm grateful to be almost done with these stupid meetings, because I was sick of them about five seconds after the first one began. But it also means that Jenna and I will soon have to part ways again.

I try not to think about the moment that this arrangement will be over for good. But it's coming closer and closer no matter what. When she's finally knocked up and doesn't need me anymore ... I don't know what I'll do.

The meetings drag on until I start to wonder if someone sabotaged all the clocks in the room. Finally, the representatives from the distribution company rise to their feet and say good-bye, and I tear out of there like my ass is on fire.

I head back to the hotel and walk into our room with a weary sigh of relief. "Thank Christ *that's* all over. You have no idea how glad I am to be ba—"

Jenna looks up from the vanity mirror where she sits

with her hairbrush in hand. I stop to admire the view she's so generously treated me to. She's wearing heeled boots and a long suede skirt in deference to the crisp weather, but her top half is adorned with only a lacy black bra.

She quirks her eyebrow at me, smirking ever so slightly. "I take it you like what you see."

"I always do." I lean against the wall and flash her a lewd grin. "Don't stop on my account. Go on, I'll just enjoy the show."

She finishes brushing her hair and picks up one of the many makeup jars and palettes scattered in front of her. "As you can see, I'm running late getting ready for dinner."

I tilt my head. "You do your hair before putting on your shirt?"

"I left it for last so I wouldn't get makeup all over it. Women do that." She starts brushing beige powder all over her face.

"Hmm." It makes sense. I just never would have thought of it on my own. I've seen plenty of women dressing or undressing, but never readying themselves for a date. I realize that I kind of like seeing Jenna this way. It feels oddly . . . intimate. Domestic.

After I've watched her put on blush, eyeshadow, and lipstick, I ask, "Where do you want to go tonight? If you don't care, I was thinking steak." I'm in the mood for seared cow, and I feel like treating Jenna to someplace upscale.

"Steak sounds great. Do you know a good place?" She blinks as she carefully applies mascara.

"Not really, but we can ask the front desk."

She stands up. "There, I'm done. Sorry for the wait." She leans toward the bed to pick up a dark red blouse.

"Wait." I cross the room and reach out to caress her breasts through her bra.

She sucks in her breath almost too quietly for me to hear. Almost. "H-hey . . ."

I bend down to kiss first one breast, then the other, and straighten up to peck her on the cheek, careful not to smudge her makeup. "All right. I'm satisfied . . . until later tonight."

She laughs, though her cheeks are a little pinker than before. "Okay, horndog, I'm putting the boobs away now." She shrugs into the blouse and buttons it up.

After asking the concierge for a recommendation, we get into a cab and head to what he claimed was the best steakhouse in the area. We both order bacon-wrapped filet mignon medallions and quickly absorb ourselves with flirting, debating about books and movies, and retelling funny anecdotes from our younger years. I love the way her sharp tongue and even sharper wit keep me on my toes. The waiter's return barely breaks our stride; we keep chatting and laughing as we eat, completely comfortable together.

Jenna always has a way of lifting the weight off me, and by the time we've finished our meal, the stress from work has drained away. All I needed was some good company, good food, and easy conversation. Well, maybe this isn't *everything* I need—I definitely plan to follow up on that flirting in bed tonight.

As I polish off my last bite of tender beef, I ask, "Have you enjoyed the trip?"

She nods with a bright smile. "Definitely.

Everything's been great. The library, museums, the hotel spa." She makes a little noise of pleasure at that last one. I was happy to pamper her. She'll be pregnant soon and certainly deserves it. "And I've worked a little during the day too on my laptop, and checked in with my assistant and the shop."

I nod. "What do you want to do with the rest of our last night?"

She considers it. "You've been to New York before, right? Surprise me."

I rub my chin. "How about we start with dessert? I know a restaurant that sells nothing but artisan cheesecake in little jars."

Her eyes light up so dramatically, I have to laugh.

"Guess I picked the right suggestion," I say, teasing her.

She pokes her tongue out at me with a grin. "What are we waiting for?"

At the next restaurant, we stuff ourselves silly sampling all the different flavors: turtle, blackberry, green tea, lemon ginger, red velvet, and salted caramel apple. Afterward, we visit an art museum, where Jenna excitedly points out the Greek, Roman, and Byzantine influences in every painting and sculpture. Then it's off to a speakeasy where we drink French cocktails and sway together to a live jazz band. Playing the night by ear, we go on a whirlwind adventure through New York City's nightlife, hopping from bar to club to gallery, ending with a leisurely people-watching walk through the city streets as we wind our way back to our hotel.

The instant the door clicks shut behind us, I pull her into the bedroom for a hungry kiss. Still devouring her mouth, I unbutton her skirt and let it fall to pool on the floor around her feet. I nudge her backward to sit on the bed, then finally break the kiss to kneel. Too impatient to finish undressing her, I pull aside her panties and dip my head low, inhaling her heady scent before my tongue slips out to taste her. Jenna stifles a groan as she runs her hands through my hair, gripping to hold me in place. I love that groan.

My cock strains painfully at my zipper as I slowly lave her clit and tease her opening with my fingertips. Jenna stares down at me, her cheeks red and pupils dilated, captivated by the erotic sight. Then I flicker my tongue in the exact way I've learned drives her wild, and she falls back flat on the bed with a whimper, her hands clutching at my shoulders and head. I suck on her clit and hum, knowing what the vibration will do to her.

"Emmett," she cries, her nails scraping along my scalp like she's trying to hold on.

I lap at her like I'm dying of thirst, drunk on her sweet honey, unable to get enough of her. Her hips twitch and grind up into the stimulation. Her cries pitch higher, louder, and then suddenly she gasps and her thighs clamp down around my head so hard they quiver. Her pussy pulses rhythmically against my lips and chin. I don't stop licking until she chokes, "S-stop. Oh, *fuck* . . ."

Still breathing hard, she sits up and bends in half to kiss me. In my lust-fogged state, it takes me a second to realize that she's fumbling at her blouse buttons.

"Hang on," she mutters.

"Screw the shirt, the boots too. Just come here."

I lie on the bed and lift a half-naked Jenna in my

arms. She straddles me, unzips my dress pants, and sinks down on my cock. I groan aloud in ecstasy. As much as I love her mind and spirit, the baser side of me also loves fucking her bare, and I don't know how I'll ever go back to using condoms with the one-night stands I pick up at bars.

Jenna rides me hard, pounding me into the mattress, and I buck up to meet her with every plunge. My fingers grip her, helping her move as my thumbs work furiously at the firm, slick bud. Her thighs tremble with exertion and mounting pleasure. I can't get enough of her. In moments like this, everything else falls away. She becomes my whole world and I want nothing more than to keep her in my bed forever, to make her feel so good that she'll never even think about leaving me. My fingers dig bruises into her hips as stars burst white over my vision, and I empty myself inside her. With a little encouragement from my hands, she falls apart a second later, moaning as her inner muscles spasm around me.

Slowly, almost reluctantly, she lifts off me, and I feel a pang of loss when the last of my cock slides out. She tugs off the rest of her clothes and lies naked on her side next to me. With a dreamy sigh, she drapes her free arm and leg over me and cuddles close.

I don't want to disentangle myself from her, even just for the moment it would take to get undressed. I pull her into a secure embrace, my bliss already tinged with melancholy. Some premonition, some gut instinct warns me that the first month was a fluke and she's sure to become pregnant this time. And then . . .

And then she won't need me anymore. I will have outlived my usefulness at that point. The thought is sobering.

My arms tighten around her. The thought of letting Jenna go is intolerable, and I have no idea what I'm going to do. I push away the urge to talk to her about this. There wouldn't be any point. I know there's no solution to be found . . . no way to make this relationship work. Dragging our incompatibilities out into the open would just pour salt in my wounds.

But God, they hurt already. I ache every time I think about her.

I lie there in the dark, holding a woman I didn't know I wanted, that I can never have, listening to the soft rhythm of her breath as I try to quiet the doubts starting to swirl through my head.

Chapter Seventeen

Jenna

Work has been hell, with mounting financial problems and the increasingly pushy buyout offers from my competition. But I can't bring myself to care about that right now. The moment of truth, the moment I've been hoping and praying and fretting over for so long has finally arrived. It's time to see if all my—no, our—efforts have paid off. And I can't stand waiting another second for my doctor's appointment tomorrow afternoon.

After work and a trip to the drugstore, I text Emmett, *I bought a pregnancy test.* I actually bought three, just to make sure.

He replies almost immediately. *Don't take it yet. I'll be there in twenty minutes.*

Since I've waited six weeks—or more accurately, my whole life—I decide I can wait another twenty minutes. It's sweet that Emmett's almost as excited about this as I am.

I try to read a magazine, give up because I can't focus, and pace rapidly around my apartment until I hear his knock.

I open the door and gesture him inside. "Thanks for coming."

"Of course. I wouldn't miss it." He pulls me in for a brief hug, and instantly, I feel a little calmer. "Are you nervous?"

I chew on my lip and nod. "It should only take a few minutes until I know one way or the other."

"I'll be right here." He perches on a bar stool in the kitchen with an attentive expression.

I'm grateful for his presence, which seems to ground me. "Wish me luck." I press a kiss to his cheek and head toward the bathroom.

I reread the instructions for the fifth time just to make sure I don't mess this up. Okay . . . pee in a cup, dip the test's tip for five seconds, remove it, wait three minutes. That's easy. I can totally do this.

After following the instructions, I set the test on the

bathroom counter and remind myself to breathe. The seconds tick past at a glacial rate, but finally, something starts to happen. With maddening slowness, one pink line appears . . . then two!

"Holy shit," I say out loud.

"What?" Emmett calls, his voice muffled through the door.

He sure didn't stay sitting for long, but if he feels even half as keyed-up as I do, I can't blame him.

"Hold on." I rip open the other two boxes and use them too.

"Hey, what's going on in there? The suspense is killing me."

"Just one more minute." I can barely contain myself as I wait for the tests to turn out. Was the first result a mistake, a fluke?

But no . . . the other two show double lines too. I fling open the bathroom door, spot Emmett, and throw my arms around his neck in glee.

"I'm knocked up!"

His face lights up. "Really? You're pregnant?"

I nod, grinning so hard my cheeks ache. "All three tests were positive." Then I squeal when he sweeps me into his arms with a sound of joy and twirls me around. We pepper each other with kisses, ecstatically bear-hugging, laughing in sheer excitement.

He sighs, looking into my eyes with tender pride. "We actually did it. How do you feel?"

"We did." I plant a firm kiss on his lips, tears brimming in my eyes. "And I feel . . . incredible."

When my stomach ruins the moment with a gurgle, he chuckles. "What about hungry?"

I laugh. "I'm not eating for two yet."

"I asked about you, not the baby," he says. "I worry about you sometimes. Knowing your workaholic tendencies, I'm guessing you haven't eaten dinner yet."

"You calling me a workaholic? Do I even have to say pot, kettle, black?" I poke the tip of my tongue out at him. "But . . . you got me there. No, I haven't. I came straight home from work to take these tests."

We order a Chinese-food feast and spread our army of paper boxes over the little dining table in my kitchen. As we dig in, silence falls ... and with it creeps a slow melancholy that tempers the joy of my success.

Now what? The question nudges insistently. But how will he answer if I ask? Emmett promised me he didn't want any part in raising a child and said he'll happily get out of my way once I'm pregnant.

Hell, at the beginning, that's exactly what I asked him to do. We were once on the same page, but since then my feelings have drifted so far. I still don't know if I can handle a serious relationship ... yet at the same time, now that I'm about to lose him, I realize just how desperately I wish otherwise.

I try to push away my unspoken, unspeakable doubts and make small talk. But it's halfhearted, and Emmett answers in monosyllables, clearly preoccupied. Eventually, I give up and we eat our chicken chow mein in silence.

When the takeout boxes are empty, I crack open my fortune cookie. "Enjoy the good luck a companion brings you," I read aloud. "That's accurate. You've definitely brought me luck."

He gives me a half smile that seems oddly tense. "Glad to hear it."

"What did you get?"

He opens his cookie and frowns at the tiny paper slip. "'A dream you have will come true.' Well, that's vague as hell." Then, looking away from me, he says, "It's getting late. I guess I should get out of your hair."

What can I say except, "All right?"

As I walk him to the door, our eyes meet and I hesitate. *Don't go* teeters on the tip of my tongue. Maybe a quick, formal farewell is the right thing to do ... but I can't bring myself to leave things at that. If this is my last chance to touch Emmett, I'll never forgive myself if I don't take it. I lean up to kiss him good-bye for the last time, wrapping my arms around his solid shoulders and breathing in the scent of his crisp cologne.

A small noise of surprise escapes him before his arms close around me tight and his hand cradles the back of my head. For a long moment I linger, savoring the feel of his lips, his solid body, trying to imprint it into my memory so I'll never forget—so I can carry at least that small piece of him with me.

He pulls away slowly, as if he, too, feels reluctant to part. "I . . ." He takes a breath. "Um, if you want to keep me posted about how the baby is doing, how you're doing with the pregnancy, I . . . would like that."

"Oh?" I blink, then smile. "Okay. I will."

I watch him walk away down the hall. Only when the elevator closes behind him do I shut my door. I turn out the lights, brush my teeth, and change into pajamas. Then I lie down in bed, stroking my still-flat belly, wondering what the future holds and how I'll fare as a mother . . . and how it will feel to let go of Emmett, the father of my unborn baby.

Dammit, this is stupid. I've done exactly what I set out to accomplish. My hard-won success has finally arrived. So, why can't my heart get with the program? Why, under all my excitement and nervousness and pride, do I feel so down?

I know why. But I still try to convince myself that my weird mood is just a standard case of pregnancy jitters.

As I snuggle under the covers, I place the call I've

been waiting to make for a long time. "Hey, Mom," I say when she answers.

"Tell me some good news, baby girl."

"You're going to be a grandma," I say, my throat tight.

When she lets out the biggest squeal of joy I've ever heard, tears spring to my eyes.

We talk for a while longer, all about baby names and birthing plans, until the conversation shifts to the sperm donor I chose. I don't know how to tell her about Emmett. Don't know how to explain him and his role at all. Yes, he was my donor, but he feels like more. Instead, I make an excuse about needing to get ready for bed and end the call.

A ding interrupts my conflicting thoughts. I check my phone to find a text from Emmett.

Make sure not to eat any raw fish from now on. I'm sure you already knew that, but just saying.

My lips twitch up. *Of course*, I reply.

Another text appears almost instantly. *And don't sleep on your back.*

That's not until I'm much further along, I type back, my smile growing.

Yet another message. *Did your doctor recommend you take any prenatal vitamins?*

He keeps texting me little tips and factoids and questions until it gets so late, I have to say good night.

I turn off my phone and snuggle under the covers, feeling a little more cheerful. Even if we're not sleeping together anymore, maybe I won't have to say good-bye to his friendship after all.

Chapter Eighteen

Emmett

It's been two weeks since Jenna's pregnancy tests came out positive. Two weeks since we were together. And I'm slowly but surely losing my damn mind. I'm pretty sure half of my staff is ready to quit with how on edge and snappy I've been.

Although I'm dying to see her, I have no convenient excuse to call, now that we've succeeded at the entire reason we started sleeping together. I would have to come out and admit that I just want to be near her and ask if she wants that too. And I already know that leap of faith wouldn't end anywhere happy. We're both so independent—we'd probably never work—yet I'm having a hard time remembering why.

But, damn, I can't deal with this much longer. I can't even seem to relieve tension by myself. At some point, I realized that if she doesn't need me to have a high sperm count anymore, my dick belongs to me again. That I can go back to jacking off whenever I want. But the first time I tried, I ended up stopping after a few halfhearted minutes because it wasn't any fun—and I haven't bothered with it since. I don't want to use my own hand, alone in an empty penthouse. What I want is Jenna, but she's slipping further away by the day.

Trying to convince myself that she still needs me, that our connection doesn't need to be broken just yet, I started obsessively researching pregnancy. I ordered books online and had them shipped to me overnight. I read medical articles and mommy blogs in my office while I was supposed to be working. What started as an attempt to quiet my neurosis soon backfired, though, because I became genuinely terrified of all the dangers lurking in pregnancy.

Jesus Christ. I'm perched on my sofa after work, my eyes glued to my latest purchase, speed-reading a litany of bloodcurdling hazards. Gestational diabetes, pre-eclampsia, early labor, infections, a thousand other potential complications.

No wonder "died in childbirth" is such a cliché of old tragic stories. How the fuck has the human species survived this long when there are so many things that can go horribly wrong with reproducing?

I force myself to put the book down and try to calm

my breathing. This is only driving me further down the rabbit hole than I already am. *She's perfectly healthy*, I tell myself firmly. Hell, I'll prove it. I grab my phone and text Jenna, *Are you feeling well?* There. I'll hear straight from the horse's mouth if anything is wrong, but there definitely won't be, so I have no reason to lose my marbles.

I can't sit still. I pace around my living room until she replies, *I'm fine.*

Shit . . . that was the exact response I hoped for, but it doesn't calm me down at all. I text her back, *Are you sure? Any pain, nausea, fatigue? Cravings? I can swing by the store later if you want me to pick something up.* Some distant part of my mind whispers that I'm acting like a lunatic and I need to back off, but I can't stop myself.

No, I promise, she replies, *I'm totally fine. Relax, Emmett.* I can just picture her expression right now, amused with a touch of gentle exasperation.

"See?" I say out loud. "You heard the lady. Chill out."

Then my phone buzzes again. *Except . . .*

The bottom drops out of my stomach. *Except what? What is it?* I rush to type back.

A minute, then, *Never mind, it's no big deal.*

I almost let out a hysterical laugh. Holy shit, she can't just backpedal on me like that. *Please tell me what's wrong before I have a panic attack.* I type frantically, correcting a myriad of typos as I go.

Sorry. Didn't mean to worry you. It's just . . . you've obviously been doing some research, did you come across anything about increased libido during pregnancy?

I stare at her words for a moment, reading them over and over to make sure I understand what she's asking . . . then I close the message and call her. I can't handle this conversation through text. I need to hear her voice—not to mention talk without anxiety-inducing pauses between every sentence while I await a response.

As soon as she picks up, I answer her question. "I did see mentions of that, actually."

"Oh, thank God." She sighs. "I'm so horny, and I thought I was losing my mind. But I guess this is just normal."

"Huh," I mutter. It seems a little early for that symptom to appear. I thought it wasn't supposed to start until late in the first trimester. But everything I've read says that every pregnancy is a little different, and this doesn't seem dangerous.

I'm sure as hell not complaining about the chance to touch her again. I thought that door had closed two weeks ago, and here I am standing right in front of it again. She needs me, but not for my sperm this time. That ship has sailed. She needs my dick for much bigger reasons ... possibly nine months of bigger reasons. My dick is very happy at this turn of events.

"Huh, what?" she asks.

"Nothing." My mood much improved, I say, "I was just thinking I know exactly how to help with your little problem. Hell, I can drive over right now if you want."

"Is that a good idea?" She sounds uncertain. "Shouldn't we keep our distance?"

"Fuck that. Listen, if you're mentioning it to me, I'm guessing that masturbation isn't doing it for you anymore, right?"

"Uh . . . no," she admits quietly.

"So you need a man, and I'm well-qualified for the job. I mean, we know we work well together. Besides, I'm not about to let you go off around the city picking up strangers who will do God knows what to you and the baby. It's a safety issue, really." That concern isn't a complete lie. I'm just not mentioning my other two motivations—the overwhelming desire to see her and touch her again, and the idea of her fucking another man makes my blood boil. "I know that knocking you up was all we explicitly talked about, but it's also my job to make sure you get the baby you want. So, protecting you both comes with the territory."

I resist the urge to add *and this is my baby too*. That's not what we agreed to. That's not what it says on all the legal paperwork we signed. *My baby* was never part of the legalese; it was always her child. But that knowledge, that biological reality, nevertheless draws me in with irresistible force.

She pauses for so long, I start wondering if my phone lost signal. "All right," she replies at last, and there's a softness in her voice that does strange things to my insides. "Are you sure you don't mind?"

I almost bark out a laugh. *Mind? Getting another chance to have sex with her? She's obviously already suffering from pregnancy brain.* "Not at all."

"Then come on over, big boy, and I'll put you to good use."

I hustle to the car so fast, I almost forget my keys.

At her apartment, she answers my knock right away. She looks tired, is wearing stained sweatpants and a baggy T-shirt, and all I can think is, *God, how can a woman be so beautiful? How have I stayed away from her so long? Is this the pregnancy glow, or am I just a smitten fool?*

And most importantly, *What the hell was I about to say?*

"Hey," she says, her voice soft.

Jenna's messy ponytail makes her look even younger, and I have to physically resist the urge to cup the back of her neck and use it to pull her in for a kiss.

"How are you feeling?" I ask, stepping inside as she closes the door behind me.

"Good. Great, actually." Her lips twitch with a smile, and God, it's so fucking good to see her.

I pull a small plastic bottle out of my coat pocket. "I bought you these prenatal vitamins from the drugstore. The books I've been reading said you should start tak—"

"Later. Come here." And she yanks me by the lapels into a ravenous kiss that makes up for every lonely moment of the last two weeks.

• • •

Jenna flops back onto the pillow with a sigh of exhausted satisfaction. "Whew . . . I really needed that."

Me too, I don't say. "Glad I could lend a hand." I smirk at her. "And a tongue, and several other body parts."

"Shut up," she says with a chuckle. She scoots over to rest her head on my chest, her arm draped over my waist, and for a long, blissful while, I just stroke the soft skin of her back and listen to her quiet murmurs of pleasure. I haven't felt so relaxed and content since the last time we shared a bed.

Just when I think she's fallen asleep, she mumbles, "Hey, do you want to order a pizza?"

Come to think of it, I haven't had dinner yet. I was too engrossed in reading, and then in rushing over here so I could make Jenna scream. "I could eat. Anywhere you're in the mood for?"

She makes a noncommittal noise. "Doesn't really matter to me. Whatever's open at this hour will have to do."

"Hmm . . ." I really don't feel like letting go of Jenna. "How about Mama Jo's?"

"Sounds good to me. Who's going to be the one to put on pants to answer the door?"

I laugh. "I'll do it."

"But that means I have to stop lying on you," she points out.

"Shit, you're right." I ponder. "Well . . . we have until the pizza gets here. And then you can get right back on me again."

I call the pizza place, order a large pepperoni with mushrooms, and bring it back for us to eat in bed once it's delivered. After we've each polished off a slice, Jenna says, "So . . . getting together tonight turned out to be a great idea. You want to keep doing this? For as long as I'm able to, that is."

I suppress the urge to fist pump and holler *hell yes*, opting instead to reply as casually as I can manage, "If it helps you, of course I do."

I know this only pushes our relationship's expiration date out a little further, but still . . . there are no words to describe how relieved and happy I am for this stay of execution. Hopefully, Jenna will continue to enjoy my company for the next eight months.

We eat and chat about nothing, just like old times, until the box is half-empty and neither of us can fit another slice in our stomach. When I come back from putting the leftovers in her fridge, I find that Jenna has fallen asleep sitting up.

I stifle a laugh. She must have been worn out. I hope I can take that as a compliment to my sex skills, because the alternative is that she's been working way too hard.

Careful not to wake her, I tug the blanket up over her and turn off the light. Then I just gaze at her peaceful face for a few moments, unable to force myself to walk away. Of course, all the books I've read said that the first trimester is the most exhausting with hormones and a baby growing inside her . . . but I'll let her sleep with the knowledge that I sexed her so good and that's why she's fast asleep.

But I don't want to leave. I want to fall asleep holding her in my arms, wake up with her beside me, maybe get breakfast together if there's time before work. But she didn't specifically invite me to stay the night, and even though we've already shared a hotel bed a few nights, sleeping over at her place feels like crossing a more significant line.

So, reluctantly, I give her a good-night kiss on the forehead, turn off the lights, and let myself out, but not before staring longingly at her belly, knowing that we have a child growing inside there . . . a child I shouldn't want to want.

It's becoming harder to convince myself that I'm still that same non-father-material person who met her in the elevator a couple of months ago.

Chapter Nineteen

Jenna

At four weeks pregnant, it's time for my first prenatal appointment. I wait patiently as the nurse checks my height, weight, pulse, blood pressure, and temperature, then takes blood and urine samples. I already gave a complete medical history the first time I came here, but she asks me the entire survey again, with bonus questions about Emmett, until I've recited what feels like every cough and headache our families have ever suffered for generations.

Finally, she hands me a paper gown. "Change into this and lie on the table, please. The doctor will be in shortly to do your pelvic exam." Then she leaves me alone for the first time in almost an hour.

Whew ... I knew when I started trying for a baby that I was signing up to become a lab rat, but this level of scrutiny will take some getting used to. And I'll be repeating it more and more frequently until the day I give birth. Hopefully, next time won't be so intense, now that we've established a baseline for my health.

I unfold the paper gown, cover myself the best I can,

and lie down just as someone knocks on the door. "Come in," I call out.

Dr. Kaur bustles into the exam room. "Nice to see you again, Miss Porter. How are you?"

"I'm fine, you?" I reply automatically.

"Good, good." She washes her hands at the sink before joining me near the exam table. Unfolding the paper that's covering me, she explains her movements as she goes. "Now I'll just check for lumps here . . ." She squeezes my breast and I wince slightly. "Tender?"

"A little. I assume that's normal."

"Yes, but still, I apologize." Moving much more gently, she continues interrogating me as she works. "Do you smoke or drink?"

"I've never smoked. I used to have one or two drinks occasionally, but I stopped as soon as I knew I was pregnant."

She hums an approving murmur. "Exercise?"

"I go to the gym twice a week." Or I try to, anyway. Hopefully, a tiny bit of exaggeration isn't a medical sin.

Besides, sex is a form of exercise, right?

"Feet in the stirrups, please. I'm just going to take a look at your cervix."

"Will you bring me back a souvenir?" I joke as I prop my legs up.

She gives the tiniest possible huff of polite laughter. "Ideally, I'll find nothing there. Now, you might feel a slight pinch."

Lies, all lies. It feels like she's digging around for buried treasure, and I resist the urge to flinch. *Ow* . . . is it really necessary to crank that thing open so wide?

While she pokes and prods around, she asks, "Any significant sources of stress?"

Well, a person in a lab coat is currently barking questions into my vagina, so . . . "I've been having some trouble with work lately, but nothing unusually stressful." Trying to keep the Lit Apothecary afloat has been an adventure right from the word *go*.

Oh yeah . . . and figuring out what the fuck I'm going to do about Emmett. I still don't have a good answer to that one. For the sake of my sanity, we've kept sleeping together, and he gets my hopes up by doing sweet things like texting me things he's researched about the pregnancy, even when he doesn't have to. But all that has to end eventually, right?

Hell, I don't know. And I don't even want to think about it. What's that saying, ignorance is bliss? In this case, ignoring it has been bliss, so I'm just going to keep on ignoring the situation between the two of us.

I breathe a subdued sigh of relief when Dr. Kaur finally finishes and steps outside to let me get dressed. When I'm decent again, she returns and sits at the computer. She scrolls down for a minute, skimming the nurse's notes. "You mentioned that your partner's grandfather died of cancer. Do you know what kind? And how old he was?"

"Uh . . ." I glance at the typed packet in my lap. I interrogated Emmett about his medical history in anticipation of this visit, but I'm drawing a blank. "Sorry, I don't."

"Hmm." She frowns over her glasses at me. "All right." She swivels around to the screen for another minute, then back to me. "Have you noticed any problems or irregularities since your last period?"

I shrug. "None that come to mind. I've felt pretty great."

She blinks owlishly behind her thick lenses. "Really? No nausea, heartburn, fatigue, dizziness, headaches, mood swings, constipation, spotting, cramping, trouble sleeping, food cravings or aversions . . ."

I shake my head at most of the symptoms she rattles off. "Nothing except for maybe a little fatigue and . . . uh, an increased libido."

"Excellent." She favors me with a rare smile. "It seems pregnancy suits you."

I grin back at her. "I hope so. What comes next?"

"We're going to perform a pelvic ultrasound. Would you like to hear your baby's heartbeat?"

I give her an enthusiastic nod.

An ultrasound tech wheels in a machine, and Dr. Kaur stands back as the screen soon comes to life with a blurry black-and-white image of a bean-shaped baby, and the best *thump-thump-thump* noise I've ever heard.

Tears fill my eyes as I watch the screen in wonder. This moment is even more than I ever dreamed it could be. God, how I wish Emmett was here, holding my hand, seeing what we've done.

"Everything looks perfect, Miss Porter," the ultrasound tech says as she finishes.

"You and your baby seem to be in perfect health," Dr. Kaur adds. "Speak with the receptionist to schedule another prenatal checkup in four weeks."

"Oh, that's such great news," I say on a relieved breath. I didn't even know how much tension I was carrying until I got to see the baby with my own eyes.

"What questions can I answer for you?" Dr. Kaur may be on the brusque side, but she knows what she's doing and takes me seriously.

"Um, do you know when I'll be due?"

"Oh, right." She pulls out a calendar and consults it. "I estimate your due date to be in mid-August of next year. We'll refine that estimate as we get closer." She holds out her hand. "If I haven't already said so, congratulations. I'm happy for you."

Beaming, I shake her hand. "Thank you."

As I step out of the building into the thin, wintry sunlight of late afternoon, I pull out my phone to call Emmett. "The doctor said everything looks great," I tell him.

"That's wonderful news," he replies, sounding genuinely enthused, and I can't hold back a giddy grin. "What are your plans for the rest of the day?"

"I was going to drop by the mall and check out what their baby stuff is like, and then figure out dinner." I unlock my car and get in.

"Want some company? I'm still at work, but I was thinking of calling it a day soon, and there's nothing to do at home."

I should seriously think about this, but *fuck it*. "Sure. Meet me by the food court entrance?"

"I'll be there in half an hour. I just need to wrap up

here."

"Okay, see you soon." I hang up and head downtown.

•••

Emmett meets me right on time, and together we stroll through the mall to an adorable baby boutique I've never let myself enter, not wanting to get my hopes up.

"Now, remember," I warn him as we enter, "you're not allowed to tell me what I should or shouldn't get."

"Got it. No opinions on anything." He mimes zipping his mouth shut and throwing away the key.

I smile at that, appreciating his ease at letting me do things my way and call the shots. Pausing by a shelf of crib blankets, I pick up one to stroke the cloud-soft fleece and consider its pattern of dove-gray geometric stripes. "Oh, cute," I muse.

Emmett looks over my shoulder. "I like it."

Forgetting I'm not supposed to care what he likes, I glance back at him. "Really?"

"Yeah. We don't know if we're . . . I mean, if you're having a boy or a girl, so it's good to get something gender-neutral. Though I'd have a hard time choosing between this and that one." He points at a buttery cream-colored blanket.

I examine it and find myself in agreement. "Yeah . . . they're both such good colors. Darn, you've made my decision harder."

He chuckles. "Sorry."

"I think . . . I don't know why, but something tells me it's going to be a girl. Still, though, it's good not to color-code everything. I grew up surrounded by so much pink, I hated it on principle until I was a teenager."

"We could buy blue just to fuck with people," he suggests.

I laugh. "No, it's not worth constantly explaining the joke to people."

He grabs another blanket, this one striped in seafoam and olive. "What about green?"

"Stop giving me more good options or we'll be here

all night," I say with a mock groan.

"Are you going to find out the sex?"

"Yes. And, oh my God, I forgot to show you these pictures of the baby." I pull the black-and-white printouts from my purse and hand them to Emmett.

His face twists in wonder and he blinks, a slow smile uncurling on his mouth. "Holy shit."

"I know." I grin back. "And I heard the heartbeat."

Swallowing once, Emmett hands the pictures back to me. "It's incredible, Jenna. I'm so happy for you."

As we wander through the store, examining and debating toys, strollers, clothes, furniture, nursery decorations, and every other kind of baby accessory under the sun, we find ourselves agreeing on almost everything. Our tastes line up perfectly. It feels so *right*, so dangerously good to run such a domestic errand with him—to act like parents together.

I shouldn't let myself wish this was real, but longing floods my imagination and I can't fight the pull. I picture Emmett becoming part of my life, *our* lives, always nearby.

Smiling down at his newborn daughter as he cradles her tiny body in his arms. Feeding her, playing with her together, rocking her, even changing her is all so cozy and welcoming in my mind's eye. It's love. It's home.

I break away from Emmett in the stroller aisle, brushing off his concerned questions with a terse "I'm fine, just need to pee," and hide in the restroom until I manage to bite back my tears.

Goddamn it, I hate this. I never wanted to want any man so badly. I knew better, tried to avoid it, yet I've still fallen for someone who will leave me. And I can't do jack shit about it. I just have to wait, helpless, as every passing day brings the end a little closer.

It takes a few minutes, but I try my hardest to calm myself down until I don't look anything like how I feel. Then I put on a smile and emerge from the restroom to rejoin Emmett ... because I sure as hell don't want to waste what little time we have left.

Chapter Twenty

Emmett

As I leave work, I find a voice mail waiting on my phone. I expect it to be from Jenna and nervously check it, hoping that whatever she needed wasn't too urgent. But it's Aubrey, my older sister, who greets me.

"Hey, little bro, I have a small favor to ask. Frank's mom fell and broke her hip, so he has to go visit her and see if she needs anything. He should be back in a day or so. Would you mind giving me a hand with the kids tonight and maybe tomorrow?"

I call her back in the car and she picks up right away. "I got your message," I say. "Of course I'll come help you out. I'll be there in half an hour."

"Thanks. I owe you one." She sighs, and I can hear tiny voices hollering in the background.

"It's no big deal, really. I didn't have any other plans tonight." Because Jenna doesn't need me—and what if she never needs me again? That's not a road I want to go down—and the thought of sitting around my penthouse all alone sounds like torture.

I drive over to find her house in complete chaos, but

Aubrey seems unfazed, so I guess this is normal. While she nurses and bathes baby Dustin, she puts me to work juggling a bored Kimberly, a cranky Elijah, and a giggly Brooklyn who takes off running at every opportunity. Now, mercifully, all three kids sit transfixed by a Disney movie in the living room, and all I have to do is bounce Dustin on my knee while Aubrey cooks a pot of chili for dinner. But it's still total insanity.

"You were great with the little boogers," Aubrey comments over the noise of sizzling onions and ground beef.

I snort. "I managed to stop them from killing themselves or each other, you mean."

She shrugs. "Sometimes that's plenty of work on its own. Especially for four kids all under six years old. Still, I'd say you're a natural."

"Thanks?" I reply cautiously, sensing a trap.

She dumps in cans of kidney beans and crushed tomatoes. "So, how are things going with Jenna?" she asks way too casually.

And there it is. But before I brush her off with a cursory *fine*, I hesitate.

To be honest . . . I'm totally lost here, and I could use some advice. What the hell do I say, though? In the beginning, I kept my arrangement with Jenna on the down-low because we weren't supposed to ever be anything worth talking about, and now it's too late. I can't admit that she's pregnant, because my family would just think I'm a total shithead for not immediately dropping down on one knee. But I can't make an honest woman out of her . . .

Can I? Do I even want a serious relationship, let alone marriage? Does Jenna?

All I know is, I'm not ready to let go of her. It's only been five weeks and she isn't even showing yet, but I can't wait to see her with a round belly and full breasts and know that it's my baby inside her. The thought of never kissing her again, never listening to her ramble about literature and history and philosophy, never spending another night with her beside me, never holding our baby in my arms . . . it's unthinkably painful. And it's all self-inflicted. I thought I could walk away unscathed. I had no idea what the fuck I was signing up for, and now all I want is Jenna and our baby.

For the first time in my life, I want to stick around. I want to give her and the baby everything they need. I want to be part of their lives.

I swallow past a dry throat, floored by the revelation. The loud movie and the sound of Aubrey's spatula scraping the pot fill the suddenly awkward silence. She half turns to look at me, her brow furrowed in concern. "Emmett?"

I heave a loud, overwhelmed sigh. Maybe I can stick to half-truths. "I . . . really like Jenna."

Aubrey suppresses a smile. "Isn't that a good thing?"

"I really don't know. I don't think I'm at all what she wants. What do I do?"

"Well, I'd start with telling her how you feel," Aubrey says in a *duh* tone, leaning down to taste-test the chili.

I can guess why she sounds exasperated; she probably thinks my problem is just more of my typical aversion to commitment. And I can't even begin to explain all the ways this time is different. "I'm not just being dense or immature here. We had that talk in the beginning, and she's already said she's not interested in a relationship. So, what would be the point? I'd just humiliate myself and cut short what little time I have left with her."

Aubrey hums thoughtfully as she roots through the spice cabinet. "Look, I sympathize. Our parents' marriage was horrible and the divorce was even worse. After all the sh—, I mean, stuff they put us through, I don't blame you for being skittish." She throws in a generous pinch of salt and another of pepper. "But even though it's difficult—" She abruptly twists to call over her shoulder, "Sugar pie, don't grab the kitty like that, it's not nice. Don't pet him if he doesn't want to be petted." Kimberly sulks away from the cornered cat, and Aubrey turns back to the bubbling pot. "Sorry. What was I saying?"

How did she even see that? I was facing the right direction and I still didn't notice what was going on in the living room. Guess it's true what they say about parents growing eyes in the back of their heads.

"You were explaining why I'm a coward," I reply

dryly.

Aubrey's two years older than me, so she remembers that whole ugly mess even better than I do ... yet she's been happily married for ten years. She got over it somehow, and I just missed the memo. Although taking over Dad's job might have had something to do with it.

"You're not a coward. You were traumatized." She puts a lid on the pot, turns down the heat to simmer, and sits at the kitchen table beside me. "I know it's hard and scary. But the best thing to do is follow your heart. Even if Jenna says no, it's better to find out how she feels than spend the rest of your life regretting the missed chance to speak up." She reaches out to cover my hand with hers. "Don't let fear control you. Sure, people might make mistakes, but life means taking risks sometimes. And we should never stop living."

My sister's words hit me right in the chest, and I drag in a deep breath. Into her earnest gaze, I can't reply anything but, "Okay. I'll try."

I have no idea what trying involves, but I know I'm sure as hell not ready to give up on Jenna.

Aubrey beams at me and squeezes my hand before letting go. "That's the spirit. Now, you're staying for dinner, right? It'll be ready in fifteen minutes."

I don't even check my watch. "Sure, I'd love to." Going home alone is the last thing I want to do.

Chapter Twenty-One

Jenna

This careful dance we've been doing—the texting and occasional meet-ups for sex have been great, but I knew it couldn't last forever. And since I haven't heard from Emmett in a couple of days, I fear this might be the end. But then he called an hour ago to ask what I was doing this weekend, and when I replied "Absolutely nothing," our plan was hatched.

Which means I'm currently sitting alone in my apartment waiting for him to arrive. It's Friday night and the sun has just set. My mood is a bit melancholy, and I feel so unsure about everything. As excited as I've been about the pregnancy, my feelings for the man who put the bun in my oven have only grown stronger with each passing week.

Finally, a gentle knock on my door interrupts my sullen thoughts. I pull it open and find my baby daddy standing outside with a huge bunch of daisies wrapped in yellow paper in his hands.

Yellow. The color for friendship. Why does that sting so bad?

I take a deep breath and usher him inside. "Those are beautiful."

He hands me the bouquet. "I thought your place could use some cheering up."

He's right. The weather has gotten cold and gray, and there's snow in the forecast. Maybe that's the reason I've been down.

"Thank you. That was sweet. And they certainly are cheery." I head to the kitchen to fill a vase, and Emmett follows. I'd forgotten how much I've missed his warm presence, his scent.

As I place the flowers in some water, I can feel him watching me.

"Are you sure you don't want to go out and get crazy? Go to a bar, maybe? I can't even drink. I'm totally boring."

"You're my kind of boring." Emmett's mouth curves into a smile and he leans in to press a soft kiss to my lips.

I level him with a serious look. "Seriously, Emmett."

He takes my hands. "I'm not some twenty-one-year-old looking to get boozed up and laid. Actually, that last part was a lie. If sex is on the table, I'm all in." This earns him a laugh. "But, seriously, I'm almost forty. An evening in with some good company is my idea of heaven right now."

I turn from the kitchen, heading to the hall. I need a moment. It's not helpful for him to be so sweet, so sensitive, so attentive. It's not helpful for anyone. I might be fun now—but what happens when I'm nine months pregnant and huge, complete with hemorrhoids and leaky breasts? Is Emmett still going to be around then? Yeah, no. I didn't think so.

"Come here. I want to show you something," I say as he follows me.

I lead him back to what will be the baby's room. It was a home office before I rearranged everything this past week. Right now, it's little more than a dresser, boxes, and a few overfilled shopping bags. But what I really want to show him is the paint color I selected.

"What's all this?"

A drop cloth covers the wooden floor, and two

gallons of paint along with an assortment of rollers and brushes are scattered about.

"The color I chose for the nursery. It reminds me of the flowers you brought." When Emmett frowns, I ask, "You don't like the color?"

He shakes his head. "It's not that. It's just, you shouldn't be painting by yourself, Jenna. The fumes . . ."

I hold up one hand. "There's a lot I'm going to have to learn to do by myself, Emmett. Single mom, remember."

His frown relaxes and he nods again. "Right. Sorry. I didn't mean to interfere. But maybe I can lend a hand and help you paint this weekend."

"Sure."

Emmett peeks inside one of the shopping bags piled on the dresser. "You went with the gray and white." He's smiling again.

I nod. "I thought I'd decorate with gray and yellow. It's safe for either gender, and if it's a girl, I can always throw in a couple splashes of pink."

"It's going to look great." He nods to the box containing the crib that needs assembling. "I'll get that put together for you too."

I open my mouth to tell him that's not necessary, but Emmett shakes his head.

"I figure I have at least, what, seven, eight more months before you kick me out of your life. At least let me be useful till then." He chuckles like this absence in my life is funny instead of overwhelmingly heartbreaking.

God, why can't we want the same things?

On our way back down the hall, I stop in the kitchen and pick up a bottle of red wine from the shelf as Emmett enters the kitchen behind me.

"What's that?" he asks.

"For you."

He shakes his head. "You're enough, Jenna. I don't need anything but your company."

His smile makes my knees feel weak. God, why can't he be an asshole? This would be so much easier.

"Okay, then," I say, setting the bottle back onto the shelf. "So, what do you want to do?"

"Watch a movie?" he suggests.

I nod. "Actually, that sounds perfect."

We've never done something so casual, so domestic before, and I like the idea of it immediately.

We settle together side by side on my oversized sofa, cuddling together as the romantic comedy he let me pick begins.

It's only a few minutes into the movie before I'm nestling closer to Emmett, increasingly distracted by the way he looks in his dark jeans and gray sweater, by the traces of his crisp, masculine cologne.

Pressing my cheek to his firm chest, I let my hand wander to his flat stomach. My heart begins hammering away, and I hope Emmett can't tell that my thoughts have strayed from the screen and are now focused on the front of his jeans and the delightful bulge there.

If I can't give my heart what it wants, at least I can give my body what it needs—and that's more of Emmett.

I let my hand drift lower as I rub the soft material of his sweater. I venture lower still until I'm brushing the waistband of his jeans.

Emmett tenses under my touch. "Want something?"

I can't help the giggle that escapes. "Jeez. Sorry, I swear I'm not normally like a fourteen-year-old boy."

Emmett holds up both hands. "Hey, I'm not complaining."

I smile at him, feeling slightly embarrassed.

"It's true about the increased libido, huh?" he asks.

I nod. "Yes."

"I should get you pregnant more often. Who knew there would be so many perks in it for me."

It's the first time Emmett's mentioned continuing our relationship beyond this pregnancy, and for a moment my heart jumps into my throat. Then I have to tell my pregnancy brain to calm down, because it takes me a second to realize he was totally kidding.

Continuing with the task at hand, I pop open the

button on his jeans and push my hand inside to find him firm and ready for me.

"Damn, sweetheart." He grunts as my hand moves up and down, and I love watching his gaze darken with lust. "Missed this," he murmurs as he watches me slowly jack him off.

"Me too," I whisper. We kiss for a long time as I enjoy the solid feel of him in my hand.

"Tender?" Emmett asks. He cups my full breasts, rubbing his thumbs over my nipples experimentally.

I suck in a sharp inhale. "Just a little."

My body is changing. My breasts are fuller, and my clothes fit just a little differently. But so far, they are all welcome changes. The increased libido is a side effect I didn't know to expect. And the reason my—my what? Sperm donor? Friend? Baby daddy, I finally settle on—is here in the first place.

After releasing the little buttons between my breasts, Emmett draws the top off over my head as though he's unwrapping a much-anticipated Christmas present. My bra comes off next, joining my shirt on the floor beside the couch. The movie continues to play on low volume, now completely forgotten.

"Jesus, you're sexy." He brings his mouth to my breasts, cupping them in his large palms and teasing me with his tongue. "I'll be careful. Go slow. Whatever you want. But please, God, I need to fuck you."

"Yes," I murmur.

While he strips off his sweater, I stand and push down my leggings and panties so I can step out of them. It's impossible not to notice the way his gaze darkens with lust at the sight of my bare skin. He shoves his jeans and boxers down just enough to free his cock.

"You sure?" he asks, his dark eyes meeting mine.

He's always this way, checking in and making sure I'm okay, but for the first time it grates on me rather than making me feel safe. How can I tell him that no, I'm definitely not okay? I begged him for this—to put a baby inside me, and he did—but now I want things we both promised weren't in the cards for us. A relationship. Monogamy. Commitment.

"I want you," I say instead, because I do.

He brings his hand between us, teasing me and no doubt finding I'm already wet for him. Then he kisses my lips ... deep, drugging kisses, sucking on my tongue, nipping at my neck as he continues to tease little circles over my clit.

I reach down and find his cock resting on his belly. Using both hands to stroke his generous length, I return his kisses, teasing him just like he's teasing me.

"Enough," he says finally. "Ride me? I want to see those gorgeous tits bounce while you fuck yourself on my cock."

God, yes.

Shoving my feelings aside, I angle my hips while he brings himself to the needy spot between my thighs. When did I develop so many big, messy feelings? Maybe being emotional is just another by-product of pregnancy. Because right now? Gazing into Emmett's eyes, watching him let out a low groan as I impale myself on his thick length, I'm struck by All. The. Feels.

His fingers grip my hips as he rocks into me. "You

feel . . ."

I suck in a deep breath, waiting. I feel what? "Different?" I ask on a moan.

"Tighter." He grunts, pressing himself deeper inside.

Oh, right, because that's exactly what you want to hear when you're months away from squeezing a human being through your vagina.

Soon I'm rocking up and down on Emmett's stiff length, losing myself to the pleasure.

His hands on my hips guide me—slower than I would like. Normally we're frantic and hard and fast, but not tonight. He's being gentle, almost tender with me, and I'm not sure how to feel about that.

"Kiss me," I beg.

He does. And it's everything.

We make love for a long time, until he's coaxed two orgasms from me and finally reaches his own climax with a groan.

"That was perfect." He presses a final kiss to my lips

as I climb from his lap.

Once we've dressed again, we make popcorn and restart our movie.

We spend the whole weekend like that—painting the nursery, cooking, watching movies, cuddling, and making love. But we don't do the one thing I wish we could do—talk about our future. I wish I had the courage to bring it up, but the truth is, I just don't. Not when everything has been so perfect. Every part of me wishes this could be real, but the coward inside me is fine settling for the scraps.

On Sunday evening, we make homemade pasta and play a game of Scrabble. But when night falls, Emmett rises to his feet and kisses my cheek.

"I better get going," he says.

I watch his eyes, waiting to see them fill with longing or reluctance or regret. But I don't see any of those things. Instead, he pats my butt and tells me to get some sleep.

After I shut and lock the door behind him, I head to my bedroom where I promptly collapse onto my bed and sob. Wrapping my arms around myself, I lay my head on the pillow and cry for so long and hard that my breath comes in gasps and starts.

Eventually, I cry myself to sleep, something I haven't done since the night my dad left when I was a little girl.

Chapter Twenty-Two

Jenna

After my weekend spent with Emmett, it's back to reality. My eyes are only slightly puffy from my sob-fest last night, and thankfully Britt doesn't seem to notice. I've been staring at my computer screen for the last hour, trying to work up the courage for what I know I need to do.

Slowly, my stomach churning, I dial the number that that prick Ronald left me at the bottom of all his relentless emails and letters. After months of refusing to dignify his offer with a response, I can't deny the truth any longer. My little store is failing. It's been two years and I've barely kept my head above water, let alone grown the Lit Apothecary into a successful business.

In another universe, I might keep fighting until my last dollar evaporates. But here and now, with a baby on the way, I have no choice but to grow up. I won't watch my savings dwindle much lower, and I have to make the responsible decision and go back to my old unfulfilling-but-reliable job. My future family will need a steady income ... no matter how much it hurts to give up the dream I've cherished for over a decade.

I tamp down my wounded pride and press the CALL button.

"Baxter Books acquisitions department, this is Cheryl, how may I help you?" chirps a young female voice.

"Hi," I reply, wishing I was doing literally anything else. Like maybe getting poked in the eye with a sharp stick. "Can I speak to Mr. Ronald Hollenbeck?"

"Who may I say is calling?" she asks.

"Jenna Porter. I want to talk to him about . . ." I swallow the knot in my throat. "Selling the Lit Apothecary."

After a brief pause, she says, "I'll transfer your call."

"Thanks, Cheryl." As miserable as I am, I can't hold this against her.

"You're very welcome. Have a nice day." A click follows as she puts me on hold.

"I'm afraid that's impossible," I mutter into the brief

interval of empty static. I wonder if Cheryl even knows who I am. I don't know which is worse—my pain being common knowledge at their office, or the thought that I might be just one insignificant drop in a sea of faceless deals.

Soon, a nasally male voice answers with, "Ronald Hollenbeck speaking."

God, he sounds even more obnoxious than I imagined. I repeat my reason for the call, each word a fresh little stab in the gut. At least his tone isn't too smug when he says, "I can set up a meeting as soon as tomorrow at nine. Does that time work for you?"

None of this bullshit works for me, but I guess it's better to rip the bandage off as quickly as possible and get it over with. "Yes, I can do that," I reply. I make a mental note to call Britt and ask her to watch the store . . . while I sell it out from under us. *Fuck.*

"Great," Ronald says. "I'll reserve a conference room for us to discuss the sales contract. Just stop by my secretary in the morning and she'll direct you."

"Okay, thanks. See you tomorrow." I hang up and

grab a pint of butter pecan ice cream from the freezer in the break room to try drowning my sorrows in sugar.

• • •

As I turn in to the parking lot the next morning, I realize that this is the same office building as the sperm bank. I got the address off Baxter's website at the last minute, and I didn't notice that the addresses were identical except for the suite number. But I'm in too much turmoil to care about the odd coincidence. I park and walk to the entrance, then pause, trying to will myself to step through those imposing glass doors.

God, I hate this. I don't want it, I can't . . .

I steel myself with monumental effort. *There's no other way. I have to make this sacrifice for my baby's sake. I will not run away. I will not cry.* Taking a deep, shaky breath, I walk inside to sell off a piece of my heart.

I take the elevator up to the top floor and greet Cheryl, who tells me that Ronald, some lawyers, and the CEO will meet me in conference room four. I go down the hallway she points toward and find it after only a few wrong turns. As I open the door, I scan the room, looking for a free seat while taking the measure of my negotiation opponents. A bunch of pasty old men, like I expected, except for—

My heart freezes solid. *No. No fucking way.*

At the head of the long, polished oak table sits Emmett.

I almost stumble backward out of my heels. This has to be some cruel joke. Emmett's eyes have gone wide too. What's he doing here? What the hell is going on?

Before I can speak or run like hell out of there or do anything, a jowly man with salt-and-pepper hair walks through the door behind me, blocking my escape route.

"Ah, Mrs. Porter, you're here," he says.

I spin around. "Uh . . ."

"I'm Ronald. It's nice to finally meet you in person. I admit, you're even prettier than your voice suggested!" He chuckles as if he said something incredibly clever.

I finally fight off my discombobulation enough to mumble, "It's Miss, actually."

"Really? I find that surprising. Anyway, let me introduce you to our fine legal team, and of course our CEO, Emmett Smith." He gestures to a very surprised-looking Emmett.

Our CEO. No . . . this isn't a nightmare. I don't know how this is happening, but it's real. After all the sweet days and passionate nights we've spent together, now I discover we've been mortal enemies the whole time. The father of my child—the man I've fallen in love with—runs the company that's been trying to pick over the carcass of my fondest dream, and I somehow had no fucking idea. Am I an idiot? Am I insane?

Ronald waits for a second, then realizes I'm not going to respond and clears his throat. "Ah, we have a fine offer for you. We're willing to offer you a very generous price." One of the other men slides a sheaf of papers across the table. "Please let us know what you think."

Numb, I stare blankly at the contract. The insultingly low figure on its front page slaps my eyes again and again. I glance toward Emmett, who just sits there in total fucking silence.

Why isn't he saying anything? Why is he even here?

I'm going to scream and jump out the window. No, I'm going to keel over and die right where I stand. No, I'm going to puke—

Oh shit. I really *am* going to puke.

Without sparing a glance at the cluster of shocked businessmen, I bolt out into the hall and barely make it to a bathroom before I'm throwing up. Hollowed out, I cling to the cold toilet, trembling.

Someone knocks on the door. "Jenna?" Emmett calls.

"Go away," I mutter.

"Jenna, are you okay?"

"I said fuck off!" I yell, my voice cracking. Tears overwhelm me in a rush, and I curl up into a miserable ball, wracked with the all-out sobs of a child.

For uncountable minutes, I cry into the silence. Just when I start to think he's left, Emmett asks, "Can I come in?"

"What the hell do you think? How could you do this to me?" My voice rises, and I should be worried that the whole office can probably hear me, but I'm so far gone, I don't give a shit anymore. "Was this your plan all along—to put a baby in me so I couldn't fight back?"

"Of course not!" He sounds appalled. "I had no idea you owned the Lit Apothecary. Ronald was the one who handled this whole deal, and all you said was that you were in antiques and collectibles."

I don't respond. What words could possibly fix this?

Eventually, Emmett says so quietly I almost miss it, "I'm sorry. But, please, think it over. We really need this deal."

I stand on shaky legs and go to the sink. I take my sweet time cleaning myself up. Trying not to look at my red, puffy, tearstained face in the mirror, I turn on the faucet and drink from my cupped hands to wash the acrid taste out of my mouth. Only then do I reply, "Bring me the contract."

His footsteps recede, then return. He knocks again, and this time I open the door.

"Here," he says, holding out the papers, a glimmer of hope in his desolation.

I take the packet without letting our fingers brush. Then, staring Emmett square in the eye, I toss it into the toilet.

"I don't give a fuck what deal you really need. We're done." Turning my back on his shocked expression, I leave Emmett and his godforsaken vulture of a company far behind.

Chapter Twenty-Three

Emmett

Still reeling from the truth, I dismiss Ron and my legal team back to their desks and shut myself in my office. The image of Jenna's face—outraged, betrayed, *wounded*—is seared into my mind. I had no idea she owned the downtown location we're trying to buy.

I barely understand how this all happened, let alone know how to repair the damage. I desperately need advice. And at this point, it's way too late and too difficult to explain this whole complicated story to my family. So I call the only other person in my life who already knows.

"Hey, man, how you doing?" Jesse answers after a few rings.

"Pretty bad, to be honest," I say as I pull at my tie. "Do you have time to talk now?"

"Hmm . . ." A faint creak resonates over the phone, probably from him leaning back in his desk chair. "I shouldn't, but I've been beating my head against this case all morning and I need a break anyway. What's up?"

I take a deep breath and let it out slowly, thinking of

where to begin. Once I'm composed, I explain everything while Jesse listens patiently. The baby we made. The weekend trips we had. The tapas. The moment I realized it wasn't just sex. Today.

When I'm done, he lets out a long, heavy breath that mirrors my own. "You're a total idiot."

"I know." I groan. "I fucked up royally, and now I have no idea what to do. Is there even any way to fix this mess, or—"

"Isn't it obvious? Get your ass over to her place right now, apologize like you've never apologized before, and tell her you love her."

I blink. *Love.* He's right. I love Jenna. Shit. When did this happen? "Why would she give a fuck how I feel about her? Why would she even listen to what I have to say at all? She thinks I've known about this since day one, but I was just as fucking shocked as she was when she walked into the conference room."

"You have to at least try."

"She thinks I knocked her up without telling her I was trying to drive her out of business," I say, spelling it out for him. "Weren't you listening? If I were her, I'd slam the door in my face."

"It was all an honest misunderstanding. Incredibly stupid, but honest. Just explain yourself like you did to me and beg for another chance. You do want another chance, right?"

I rub my forehead. "More than anything."

"Well, there you go. Even if she doesn't return your feelings, you can try to part on good terms, or at least non-homicidal terms. And if she feels the same . . ."

"Then it still wouldn't work. My career is in the way. I wouldn't be able to be there for her like she and the baby needs."

"Calm down. It's not like having two working parents will scar a kid for life. Sheri and I have—"

"But having a CEO for a dad will," I almost shout. "You don't get it, Jesse, this job eats families. I saw it happen up close when I was a kid. My relationship with Jenna would fall apart like my parents' did, and I can't inflict that same pain on her."

"Wait, what?" Jesse sounds totally bewildered. "Is *that* why you think your parents were so fucked up? Baxter Books?" He lets out an odd bark of disbelief.

My jaw tightens. "You're seriously laughing right now? I have a real problem here, dick."

"You're right, your dick started this whole problem, remember. I'm not laughing . . . sorry. Listen, I try not to psychoanalyze people, but clearly you needed some friendly meddling a long time ago. From everything you've told me about your parents, I think it's safe to say there was a lot more wrong with their marriage than just your dad's job."

"That's what Mom always blamed," I say.

"Dude." His flat tone packs a universe of impatient incredulity into that single syllable. "Your dad was a self-absorbed, emotionally constipated douche-waffle who used workaholism to dodge his responsibilities as a husband and father. He hid behind that excuse to avoid his own family, your mom did the same to justify having affairs all over the place, and right now, you're hiding too."

"Now, wait just a—" I retort hotly.

"I get it, man. Love is fucking terrifying."

The urgent sincerity in his voice stops me cold.

"Pining and daydreaming hurts like hell, sure, but it's safe," he continues, every word punching me square in the gut. "Confessing to Jenna means facing the possibility that she'll reject you . . . or that she won't, and then you'll have to actually be her partner, with all the hard work that that entails. Hell, you'll have to be a father too. But I promise you, there's no job more important or rewarding. I know you can step up to the plate, but you have to want to, and I think you're ready."

I swallow hard but can't make it past the knot in my throat. Haltingly, I ask, "Are you sure? What if I ruin everything?"

"You won't," he replies, firm and earnest. "Just repeat after me. 'I am not my father. I can be a better man if I try.'"

"But what about—"

"Say it."

"Christ, fine, have it your way." Feeling like a dipshit, I quickly mutter his words back to him. Then I protest, "But what about Baxter Books? We needed this deal to make our quarter."

"The company won't fall apart if you stop working crazy hours . . . and even if it does, it was always destined to die, and one man pulling overtime every week wouldn't have saved it. Learn how to delegate, for fuck's sake. Hire a new VP if you have to. I'm not saying it's effortless, but balancing a career and a family can be done. Just look at me, and your brother, and your sister." He pauses. "Speaking of which, I should probably get back to this case."

"Okay. You gave me a lot to think about. Thanks for ignoring your work to talk to me." I really needed someone to have faith in me right now.

"Anytime, dude," he replies with a warm chuckle. "Good luck. Just remember what I said. And let me know how it goes."

"I will," I promise.

"If you chicken out, I'll break into your apartment

and punch you in the nuts until you talk to Jenna."

"All right, I get the message. Back to work already." I hang up and resign myself to a distracted workday of mulling over Jesse's advice.

• • •

As soon as five o'clock hits, I drive to Jenna's apartment and knock gently until she opens up. But as soon as she sees who it is, she swings the door right back again. I barely catch it before it slams shut on my fingers.

"Wait," I plead. "We need to talk. Please, just hear me out."

Her eyes flash. "Why should I? What the hell could you possibly have to say to me?" The fury in her expression stings, but not half as much as the hurt and fear, and knowing I caused it.

I take a tentative step forward. "First, let me say I'm so, so sorry. I never meant for any of this to happen. I honestly didn't know you owned the Lit Apothecary until this morning when you walked in. Everything we've done together, everything I said to you . . ." I swallow hard. "Everything I felt for you, it was all genuine. I never would have manipulated you into pregnancy just to drive you out of business."

If she thinks I master-planned this, then she truly doesn't know me at all.

"Even if you're telling the truth, it doesn't matter." Now she doesn't sound angry so much as weary. "Somehow I don't think you're going to withdraw your offer, so you're still trying to take away the business I've been dreaming of and slaving over for years. And the worst part is, I was going to let you. For the sake of my baby . . . *our* baby."

I look away in painful guilt. I have no idea what to say to that because she's right. All the apologies in the world won't change the financial reality. She needs the money and Baxter Books needs her storefront. But I can't let it all end here. There's so much more at stake, so much more that I have to tell her.

At last, I say quietly, "Jenna?"

"What?" Her voice is flat and cold and has no fight left in it.

Without breaking eye contact, I sink to my knees,

kneeling directly before her. If groveling is what it will take, I'll grovel all night.

Her eyes widen. "What are you doing? Get up."

I take her hands in mine, expecting her to jerk them away. She does flinch, clearly not expecting my touch. But she doesn't move, just fixes me with her knife-like gaze, braced and waiting to see where I'm going with this.

Looking deep into her eyes, hoping against hope that my sincerity shines through, I say, "I'm in love with you, Jenna."

She blinks. Opens her mouth, then closes it again.

"I know I said I wasn't interested in any relationship, let alone a serious relationship, and maybe it was true that day in the elevator when we first met. But the thought of going back to my old life without you . . . it's not enough for me anymore." I stroke her knuckles with the pads of my thumbs. "To be honest, it hasn't been for a long time now. I've fallen hard for you. I want us to be together . . . me, you, and the baby. And if you'll have me, I'm willing to do whatever it takes to win back your trust."

"I . . ." Her eyes are shining and she swallows hard. "But what about work, what about the offer?"

"My feelings for you have nothing to do with work. Rip up the contract, if you like. I love you. That won't change."

"Oh, Emmett." Her voice is soft, little more than a murmur, and tears fill her eyes, threatening to spill. "I want to try too."

My heart soars. I leap to my feet, but before I can sweep her into my arms, she adds in a cracking voice, "But it scares me."

"I know how you feel." God, do I ever. My heart won't slow down. I've never been so terrified in my life. "I also know that we can do this together."

She scrubs at her eyes with the back of her hand. "How? I didn't plan any of this. I don't know what to do, I—"

"Neither do I. But if we both want this, we can make it work." Remembering what Aubrey told me, I say, "There are no guarantees in life. If you're afraid to try, you'll miss all the good stuff."

Jenna chews her lip, her gaze both intent and fragile. "What about the contracts we signed? The NDA, the waivers . . ."

"I'll rip them up," I reply. "We don't need them anymore. I want to be a good father to our child. And if you'll let me try, you'll make me the happiest man in the world." I pull her to me and hug her tight.

She returns my embrace . . . then brushes her lips against mine in a featherlight, hesitant, but unmistakably certain kiss. "Show me," she murmurs.

I return it with relieved fervor. The dance of our lips and tongues turns hotter, needier, as we cling together, until I lead her to the bedroom to demonstrate just how much I intend to love her from now on.

• • •

Satisfied and damp with sweat, we curl up together, entwined amidst her tangled sheets. I can still barely believe that Jenna's given me this precious second chance, I close my eyes to savor her warmth, her feminine scent, the weight of her head over my still-racing heart. But I open them again when she props herself up on her elbow to face me, a somber turn to her full mouth.

"Listen, about Baxter Books' offer," she begins.

I shake my head. "It's your store. You can do whatever you want with it. I won't push you one way or the other."

She glances away, worrying her lip. "I admit, I'm struggling here. I have no idea what I should do. Going back to my old job is the responsible thing to do, but I've worked so hard on the Lit Apothecary."

"It's okay," I say, wanting to reassure her. "Take the deal, don't take it, whatever is best for you. Just don't do something you'll regret." I stroke her cheek with the back of my fingers. "We'll figure it out. Together. It's your choice, and whatever you choose, you can rest assured that I won't let you be unhappy. Tell me you want the moon, and I'll pull all the strings I can to make sure you get it."

Slowly, she nods, happiness blooming on her face. God, I want to see that heart-swelling smile every day for the rest of my life.

"All right," she says. "Thank you."

"Of course." I lean up to kiss her, slow and gentle.

She murmurs against my mouth, "I love you."

My stomach somersaults at her declaration. "I love you too," I answer, my voice thick with emotion.

She sighs. "Say it again."

I obey, punctuating each repetition with a peck on her cheek, her lips, and her forehead until she giggles.

Sitting up in the bed, Jenna tugs the sheet up to cover her beautifully full breasts. Then she says, "Let's go out to eat."

"All right," I say with a chuckle. "Any opinions?"

"I want . . ." Her brow furrows in concentration and confusion. "Pickles? But also cheese? And maybe chili peppers. Weird."

I laugh. "I see you've hit the 'pregnancy craving' stage. Well, how about we go back to Comal de Belén for some Mexican food? They can definitely handle spicy cheese, and maybe pickled veggies."

"Where we had our first dinner date." She grins at me. "Perfect. And you can tell Tomás you're finally settling down."

"Oh God." I groan. "He'll just find something else to hassle me about."

Still teasing each other gently, we get dressed and head out to dinner.

Chapter Twenty-Four

Emmett

Seven Months Later

"Don't push yet." I take Jenna's hand and give it a squeeze. "You can do this, baby. Just a little bit longer."

"Are you fucking kidding me?" she snaps back, her voice sharp.

Jenna rarely swears. I hate that she's in pain, but I force a pleasant smile onto my face, doing my best to keep calm. If I stay calm, maybe she'll stay calm.

"You've got this, babe. I've never been more sure of anything in my entire life."

"I don't know, Emmett." She winces again.

"Just a bit longer. I love you so much."

I'm trying to put on a brave front, but the truth is, I'm about to fucking strangle the anesthesiologist. He did Jenna's epidural an hour ago, but she's still in pain. The labor and delivery nurse is trying to be positive. She adjusts the stirrups where Jenna's feet currently rest and looks at the door again.

The door flies open and in strolls the ob-gyn who's on call—finally. He looks winded. Like he ran here.

"Sorry, folks. I hear we're ready to have a baby."

Jenna groans, and the nurse chuckles in an attempt to soothe the situation. I won't be at ease until Jenna feels better. I can't handle seeing her in pain.

"Can you do something about her pain level? I thought the epidural . . ."

The doctor waves me off. "Nothing I can do now. Everyone takes to pain meds differently. But the good news is, we're about to get the show on the road."

Once he washes his hands, the young doctor sidles up to my wife's vagina, and I have a moment where I want to punch the motherfucker square in the jaw.

"Beautiful. Fully dilated. Nicely effaced. Let's get this baby out, shall we?" He grins, and Jenna offers him a weak nod.

I lean down so my face is near hers. Sweat dots her upper lip, and I dab at it with a cool washcloth. "This is just you and me, babe. We can do this. Are you ready to meet Chloe?"

The name we picked for our little girl almost brings tears to my eyes; it's either that or the way Jenna's determined gaze locks with mine as she gives me a firm nod. She looks resolute, strong, like she can do anything she sets her mind to. And I'm certain she can.

"Let's get this damn thing out of me!" she says, groaning.

I press a kiss to her temple and hike up one of Jenna's knees while the nurse does the same with her other leg.

Now, can we just press pause on this lovely, barbaric adventure?

Because it should gross me out, right? I should be repulsed and utterly distraught by the fact that my wife is about to squeeze something the size of a watermelon out of her lovely, tight kiwi. That should be a moment I want no part of. The thing is, I'm so overcome with emotion—love, elation, pride—that tears are freely streaming down my cheeks as I watch her grunt and push and shout out obscenities.

And then the doctor is saying something about crowning, and my gaze lowers from Jenna's face to her nether-regions and, yeah, it's like a fucking bloodbath down there, like there was less blood at the Red Wedding in *Game of Thrones,* and I probably shouldn't have looked but I'm full-on crying now at the sight of my baby—our baby—emerging into this world into the hands of the doctor.

Luckily, Chloe's wails drown out my own. I lean down, burying my face in Jenna's neck. We kiss and cry and hug as they whisk the chubby pink baby away to wipe her down and weigh her.

"We did it." Jenna beams up at me. "We actually did it."

"You did, sweetheart."

And then when they place the tiny, soft little creature who has already stolen my heart onto my wife's chest, I'm hit with a fresh wave of emotion. How did I ever think that I didn't want this in my future? This is the best moment of my life—by far—and I know how incredibly lucky I am.

Chapter Twenty-Five

Jenna

Motherhood is every bit as amazing as I thought it would be, and then some.

Chloe isn't a dream baby. She fusses. She shits herself all the way up her back. She cries for no reason at all. But I love her more than words can say.

She eats and sleeps and grows, embedding herself in my heart more and more with each passing day. And Emmett? He's beyond words. I never imagined having a partner by my side, never counted on having his steady hand or sweet disposition to get me through the tough times. And, God, it's everything.

Part of me can't even believe that I ever wanted to do this alone. Sharing the joy, the sweet moments and the difficult ones too, is the best part of my day. I fucking love my husband. And believe me, I'm no domestic goddess. Sometimes it's a wonder he even puts up with me. With my hormonal crying and love of wine and need for space. But he just gets me.

And now things are about to change yet again. My

maternity leave is almost over, and quite honestly, I'm itching to get back to work. Motherhood is amazing and Emmett swears it suits me, but I'm eager to get back to my shop and a normal routine where I shower before noon and don't have leaky breasts.

The shop has never performed better. After I signed on to be part of Baxter Books, a marketing team came in and assessed my business, adding layers of marketing, PR, and advertising support. Sales have been through the roof, but I've had to take Britt's word for it.

"Honey, I'm home," Emmett's voice calls from down the hall, and my heart swells.

My everything. My rock. He's home.

"In the kitchen," I call back, tossing a container of button mushrooms into a sauté pan drizzled with butter.

I wanted to make everything tonight special, this last night of my maternity leave. I have steaks marinating in the fridge, and a bottle of merlot open and resting on the counter. Chloe is enjoying some tummy time on a nearby blanket in the living room, and her last bottle of the night is heating.

"What's all this?" Emmett asks, stopping to give me a kiss on the back of my neck.

"I was thinking we'd have a nice dinner together once Chloe went to bed."

Emmett smiles at me like he approves of this idea.

I hoped to be more put together than my usual ponytail and yoga pants by the time he got home. But, hey, the house is picked up, and more importantly, I've showered and shaved my lady bits. I think that's a win. Because, dear God, it was becoming a jungle down there.

The first time we attempted sex after I had Chloe was a disaster. It was so bad—so painful and awkward with my breast milk oozing out and Chloe crying from the other room—that we gave up and avoided the whole affair for the past few weeks.

But tonight, I'm done waiting. I want Emmett. Want to show him how much I love him. How much I appreciate him. How goddamn sexy he is. I'm going to jump my husband's bones ... I just hope our baby cooperates.

Emmett grabs two wineglasses from the cabinet and presses a kiss to my cheek. "I'm impressed. This looks amazing."

I place my arms around his shoulders, leaning into him, inhaling his scent, and smile. "I love you."

"Love you more," he says.

After he releases me, he goes to gather up our girl. I could listen to him coo and talk to her in that sweet voice he reserves just for her.

"Come here, princess," he whispers as he lifts her tiny body up against his shoulder, then he looks to me. "Should I give her a bath now?"

I nod. "And I laid out some pajamas for her upstairs."

I smile as I watch them head up to her room. There's no one I'd want by my side more than Emmett.

Epilogue

Emmett

Three Years Later

Race home and relieve the nanny? *Check*. Change from my business suit into clothes that I won't mind getting barf or dirt on? *Check*. Start a pot of soup for dinner? *Check*. Now it's time for the baby's late-afternoon feeding.

"I swear, you guys keep me busier than the office ever did," I say with a chuckle.

While I wrangle Landon into his high chair, Chloe toddles off into the living room in search of something to play with—or destroy. Our big black Newfoundland, Heidi the Second, is sleeping in the patch of sunlight by the bay window, but that doesn't last long. Chloe runs right over and yanks on her poor floppy ears.

"Be gentle, sweetie," I call out, maneuvering a spoonful of mushy peas into Landon's mouth.

Chloe doesn't really listen, but the dog clearly understands that she's only three years old. As gingerly as she would handle her own puppies, Heidi bumps my daughter backward onto her butt and licks her face while Chloe screams with laughter. Despite Heidi's hundred-pound bulk, I know my daughter is safe with her, so I let them roughhouse while I focus on trying to get more food into Landon's stomach than on his cheeks, his bib, my clothes, or the floor.

Just as I reach the bottom of the baby food jar, the garage door clunks open, then shuts. I smile at the rattle of keys. Ever since I hired a better VP and reduced my hours to spend more time with the kids, I often beat my wife home from work.

Jenna shuts the door, hangs up her coat, and toes off her pumps before walking into the kitchen to kiss me hello. "How was your day?"

"Great. How was yours?" I reply, wiping off Landon's messy face.

She heaves a tired, but happy sigh. "Crazy busy. We hosted a big reading-and-signing event this afternoon, so there was a ton of people, and before that we got in several boxes of new titles that needed shelving, but I can't really complain. Business is booming."

I nod, pleased. I used my clout as CEO to negotiate with Baxter's other executives and nudge Jenna's sales contract to something more in her favor. So, although Baxter Books became its owner on paper, the Lit Apothecary was allowed to maintain its indie charm instead of becoming the faceless behemoth that Jenna had been afraid of. She runs its day-to-day operations, and it still specializes in antique and collectible books. In fact, it's doing better than ever, now that it can draw on the marketing power of a large media company.

"Are we still on to take a walk to the park in the morning?" Jenna asks.

As Landon squeals and thrashes his tiny arms in excitement, I nod. "Sounds good to me." I poke Landon's belly, making him giggle.

Jenna chuckles. "We need to figure out where we're taking our summer vacation too."

It's a nightly dinner topic since we've yet to nail down a location. Jenna and I have already both arranged with work that we'll be gone for two weeks this summer, and we're looking forward to some time away with our mini people.

"Maybe the lava tubes of Hawaii?" I say.

She raises her eyebrows high in the pointed *you better be kidding me* look I've come to know and love so well. "You are not throwing my children into a volcano."

I wave my hand in surrender. "Fine, fine. How about camping, maybe taking the kids horseback riding?"

"Horsey!" Chloe screams from the other room, startling Heidi off her.

"Oh no, now you've done it." Jenna lets out a mock groan. "We'll have to watch that horse show *again* tonight."

I peck her on the cheek. "I take full responsibility. And I'll pour you as many glasses of wine as you want."

"That reminds me." In a sultry undertone, she murmurs, "Are we still meeting for our . . . appointment on Saturday night?"

"I wouldn't miss it for the world."

I kiss her again, this one hot and lingering. It's been

difficult to squeeze in sex between work, errands, and taking care of the kids, but so worth it. After three years and two pregnancies, Jenna is just as alluring as the day we met. Even more so, in fact, now that I've witnessed the miracles that gave her those stretch marks. Her body is so amazing, carrying our babies, carrying her through all of life's challenges, and I can't wait to see how we grow old and gray together. And our weekly date nights have definitely helped make sure we can stay connected and close.

I add, "But if you'd rather check out the inside of your eyelids, we should cancel. I'm worried you're not getting enough sleep."

"It's fine, darling." She smiles up at me through her eyelashes. "I want you too. I've been looking forward to it all week."

"Oh?" I grin. "Then your wish is my command."

She gives me one last kiss, heavy with sensual promise. "Right now my wish is dinner, a hot bath, and sleep."

"Coming right up." I lift Landon out of his high

chair and pat his back until he burps, thankfully not dribbling down my shirt. "I started some lemon chicken soup about an hour ago. It should be ready soon."

"That sounds wonderful." Jenna walks into the living room and comes back leading Chloe by the hand, an attentive Heidi trailing behind. "You ready to eat, baby girl?"

"Eat, Mama," Chloe replies as Jenna helps her into her chair at the dining table. Heidi lies down next to her, ready to gulp down any scrap of food she drops.

As I start ladling the soup into bowls, I look around my home, at my beautiful, smart, ambitious wife and my two cute, lively children, and it strikes me that I've truly never been happier.

This is a far cry from my lonely life in my penthouse apartment where every day was the same—work, gym, sleep, and more work. Each day is different, and most importantly, it's filled with people who love me.

Jenna leans past me to get our glasses and Chloe's sippy cup down from the cupboard. "What are you thinking about?" she asks.

"How thankful I am that I met you," I reply.

She pats me on the butt. "Same here."

"And I'm also glad that I stepped back to a less demanding role at work." I hesitate before adding, "Sometimes I still feel a little bit guilty about it, but I think it was the right thing to do for you and our kids."

"And for you too," Jenna says gently. "You were never a hundred percent fulfilled at that job. You're not a bad boss . . . or a bad son . . . if you don't sell your soul to the company. It's okay to take your own feelings into consideration and dial back on stuff you don't like in order to make room for what you do. You have a right to live a life you enjoy."

"I know." I set the soup bowls on the table so I can hug her. Her warm scent lingers, and it instantly calms me.

I still feel responsible for Dad's company; if I didn't, I would have found a replacement CEO long before meeting Jenna. But once I had a family, I was responsible for them too, and in a weird way, that gave me the permission I needed to change my work life like I've always wanted to anyway.

"Falling in love with you taught me that. And I've found my fulfillment right here, as a husband and father, with the people who need me most . . ." I kiss her. "And who make me happiest."

Thank God for stuck elevators and beautiful, bold women who know what they want, and cheesy spank-bank slogans that make her laugh. Thank God for good Mexican food and babies who look just like their pretty mother, and jobs that provide your paycheck but don't have to be your whole life.

Thank God for my wife. My everything.

#YouSpankIt #WeBankIt

#YouJackIt #WePackIt

Up Next

bro CODE

I didn't mean to sneak a peek of my older brother's best friend.

But when I catch him showering by mistake, I can't help but look. The guy is massive—and I do mean everywhere.

We're all home to celebrate Dad's retirement as one big happy family, except my newlywed brother's already getting divorced, my mom keeps asking why I'm still single, and most frustrating of all, Barrett Wilson is staying with us at my parents' home for the weekend.

I've known Barrett for years, so why am I suddenly noticing so many new things about him—like how big he is, and all that muscled skin and those sexy smirks? It's maddening.

Worse than that? Since he caught me looking, he uses every opportunity to tease me, handling that cucumber in the most lewd and distracting way when he's supposed to be helping in the kitchen, whispering that I could never handle a man like him.

When I sneak into his room to prove him wrong, things go from crazy to downright sinful. And it turns out, Barrett's right. There's no way I'm walking away from this in one piece.

Acknowledgments

A big thank-you to my editing team on this novel. My rock-star unicorn of an editor—Pam Berehulke of Bulletproof Editing—you rock my world. Huge thank-yous to Elaine York and Becca Hensley Mysoor, who each provided such valuable insight on this novel, and to Virginia Tesi Carey for your eagle-eye.

Thank you to my fabulous publicist and right hand in all the things, Dani—you rock my world. And a giant thank-you to my whole team—Ashley and Alyssa, I don't even want to imagine a world without you. Thank you for keeping this busy mama sane.

To my dear, sweet husband for being my everything, my reason. I am blessed beyond measure.

And last, but certainly not least—thank you to my readers. You guys are everything. I would love to hear your thoughts on *Baby Daddy*. Please leave a review at your favorite retailer, and be sure to email me your thoughts too. I love hearing from you. I can be reached at **kendall@kendallryanbooks.com**.

Get the Next Book

To ensure you don't miss Kendall Ryan's next book, BRO CODE, sign up and you'll get a release day reminder.

www.kendallryanbooks.com/newsletter

Follow Kendall

Website

www.kendallryanbooks.com/

Facebook

www.facebook.com/kendallryanbooks

Twitter

www.twitter.com/kendallryan1

Instagram

www.instagram.com/kendallryan1

Newsletter

www.kendallryanbooks.com/newsletter/

About the Author

A *New York Times*, *Wall Street Journal*, and *USA TODAY* bestselling author of more than two dozen titles, Kendall Ryan has sold over two million books, and her books have been translated into several languages in countries around the world. Her books have also appeared on the *New York Times* and *USA TODAY* bestseller list more than three dozen times. Kendall has been featured in publications such as *USA TODAY*, *Newsweek*, and *In Touch Magazine*. She lives in Texas with her husband and two sons.

Other Books by Kendall Ryan

Unravel Me

Make Me Yours

When I Break Series

Filthy Beautiful Lies Series

The Gentleman Mentor

Sinfully Mine

Bait & Switch

Slow & Steady

The Room Mate

The Play Mate

The House Mate

The Bed Mate

The Soul Mate

Hard to Love

Resisting Her

Screwed

Monster Prick

The Fix Up

Dirty Little Secret

Dirty Little Promise

For a complete list of Kendall's books, visit:

www.kendallryanbooks.com/all-books/

Made in the USA
Columbia, SC
13 June 2020